밀수록 다시 가까워지는

도서출판 아시아에서는 《바이링궐 에디션 한국 대표 소설》을 기획하여 한국의 우수한 문학을 주제별로 엄선해 국내외 독자들에게 소개합니다. 이 기획은 국내외 우수한 번역가들이 참여하여 원작의 품격을 최대한 살렸습니다. 문학을 통해 아시아의 정체성과 가치를 살피는 데 주력해 온 도서출판 아시아는 한국인의 삶을 넓고 깊게 이해하는 데 이 기획이 기여하기를 기대합니다.

Asia Publishers presents some of the very best modern Korean literature to readers worldwide through its new Korean literature series 〈Bilingual Edition Modern Korean Literature〉. We are proud and happy to offer it in the most authoritative translation by renowned translators of Korean literature. We hope that this series helps to build solid bridges between citizens of the world and Koreans through a rich in-depth understanding of Korea.

바이링궐 에디션 한국 대표 소설 058

Bi-lingual Edition Modern Korean Literature 058

So Far, and Yet So Near

이기호
밀수록 다시 가까워지는

Lee Ki-ho

ASIA
PUBLISHERS

Contents

밀수록 다시 가까워지는

So Far, and Yet So Near

1

할머니가 삼촌에게 하얀색 스리 도어 프라이드를 한 대 사준 것은 87년 가을의 일이었다.

그때까지만 해도 경기도 가평에서 혼자 농사를 짓고 살던 할머니는, 3년 동안 손수 여물을 쑤어 기른 누렁이를 판 돈에, 한여름 장날 차부 옆 약국 계단에 쪼그려 앉아 한 묶음에 천 원씩 받고 판 옥수수, 거기에 고모의 통장에 들어 있던 돈까지 모두 합쳐 총 420만 원을 마련했고, 그 돈을 미련 없이 자동차 영업사원에게 건네주

1

It was the autumn of '87 when Grandmother bought Uncle the white, three-door Kia Pride.

It was back when she still lived alone on a farm in Gapyeong, Gyeonggi-do. She sold her beloved Nureongi, which she'd personally fed for three years, and along with the money she'd saved from selling the 1,000 *won* bundles of corn on the summer market days—crouched on the stairs beside a rickety cart parked next to the pharmacy—and the money that was in Auntie's bank account, she came up with the 4.2 million *won*. Then, without even

었다. 고모가 부추긴 것도 한몫했지만, 그때 당시 할머니의 의도는 명백하고 단호한 것이었다. 삼촌이 차를 몰고 다니면, 그러면 여자가 생기지 않을까, 장가를 가지 않을까, 그것이 할머니의 예상이었다. 그래서 할머니는 그해 추석 전날, 서울 상봉동에서부터 직접 프라이드를 몰고 오느라 다섯 시간이 넘게 걸렸다고 투덜대던 자동차 영업사원에게도 군말 없이 웃돈에 송편까지 챙겨주며 등을 토닥거려주었으며, 시너 냄새가 채 가시지 않은 프라이드 유리창에 달라붙어 연신 손도장을 찍어대던 나와 사촌동생들에게는 난생처음 부지깽이를 휘두르며 '손 하나 까딱하지 마라'고 소리를 지르기도 했다. 아버지와 어머니, 작은아버지와 작은어머니는 입을 딱딱 벌린 채 그런 할머니를 말없이 바라보기만 했고, 주저주저 자동차 키를 받아든 삼촌은 다시 그런 아버지와 어머니, 작은아버지와 작은어머니의 얼굴을 힐끔힐끔 바라보며 뒤통수를 긁어댔다. 고모 혼자만 박수까지 쳐대며 삼촌의 등을 떠밀어 운전석에 타게 만들었다.

당시 서른 살이었던 삼촌은 구로동에 있는 대동피혁

blinking an eye, she'd handed the money over to the car salesman. Although Auntie had egged her on to do it, Grandmother's intentions were clear and resolute. If Uncle had a car, then wouldn't he be able to meet a girl? Wouldn't he be able to get married? That's what she'd expected. So that year, on the day before *Chuseok,* she made the car sales-man drive the Pride all the way down from Sang-bong-dong in Seoul. The salesman kept complain-ing about how it had taken him over five hours to get there, but Grandmother just patted him on the back and gave him a little extra for his troubles, along with some holiday *songpyeon* to eat on his way back up. My cousins and I scrambled up to the Pride, which still smelled of paint thinner, and put our eager little fingerprints all over the windows. For the first time in her life, Grandmother yelled at us to keep our greedy paws off and then swung a wooden poker at us. Father, Mother, Second Uncle and Second Aunt just stood there, mouths agape, staring at Grandmother. In turn, Uncle scratched the back of his head, shooting timid glances at Fa-ther, Mother, Second Uncle and Second Aunt, as he stood there with the keys in his hand.

Uncle was thirty years old then. He was living in

이라는 공장에 다니고 있었는데, 그 때문이었는지는 몰라도 열 손가락의 첫 번째 마디는 늘 갈색으로 물들어 있었다. 머리카락에선 항상 휘발유 냄새가 났고, 봄 가을 겨울, 세 계절 내내 입고 다녔던 군청색 점퍼엔 붉은색 페인트가 군데군데 묻어 있었다. 시간이 조금 흐른 후, 할머니가 경기도 가평 집을 팔고 서울 홍은동 우리 집으로 살림을 옮긴 다음부터 나는 10년도 넘게 삼촌에 대한 이야기를 듣고 듣고 또 듣게 되었는데, 어쩌면 그것 때문에 지금 여기에 이렇게 삼촌 이야기를 쓰게 된 것인지도 모르겠다(어쩌자고 어머니는 나와 할머니를 같은 방에서 살게 했을까? 아무리 방이 없다고 해도 그렇지, 이야기를 하느라 앞니가 몽땅 다 달아나버렸다고 실토하는 할머니와 재수생을 한 이불 속에 눕게 했으니, 결과는 뻔한 것이었다. 할머니는 내가 까무룩 잠이 들 때마다 어깨까지 툭툭 쳐대며 '야 야, 자냐? 웬 젊은 놈이 초저녁잠이 그리 많냐? 네 아버지가 마장동에서 한창 공부할 땐 말이다……'로 시작되는 이야기를 다시 꺼내곤 했다).

그때 할머니의 이야기에 빈번하게 등장했던 삼촌은 '이제 막 기름칠을 끝낸 경운기'처럼 하루 종일 밭을 갈고, 논을 매고, 땔감을 나르는 사람이었다. 고모가 태어

Guro-dong and working at a factory called Dae-dong Leather. Maybe that's why his fingertips were always dyed brown. His hair always smelled of gasoline and the navy blue jumper that he wore throughout spring, fall, and winter, was spotted with red paint here and there. Sometime later, Grandmother sold her house in Gapyeong, Gyeonggi-do, and from the moment she moved into our house in Hongeun-dong, Seoul, I heard the stories of my uncle, over and over again, for more than ten years. Perhaps that's why I'm sitting here today, writing down Uncle's story. (What was Mother thinking when she put me in the same room with Grandmother? Yes, there were no extra rooms, but the result was pretty obvious. Grandmother, who admitted that she'd talked until her teeth had fallen out, roomed up with an aspiring university reject. Whenever I fell asleep, she'd poke me in the shoulder and say, "Hey, hey. Are you sleeping? What type of young guy sleeps so early in the evening? Back in the day when your father was a student in Majang-dong..." And the talk would keep on going.)

Uncle, who appeared frequently in Grandmother's stories, was like a well-oiled machine, working all day plowing the fields, weeding the rice paddies, and stacking the firewood. The year Auntie was

13

난 바로 그해, 읍내 다리에서 낙상해 세상을 등진 할아버지 덕분이기도 했지만, 삼촌은 각각 아홉 살, 일곱 살 차이 나는 형님들이 서울에 있는 상고에 나란히 진학하는 바람에 읍내 중학교만 간신히 졸업한 후, 그대로 고향집에 눌러앉을 수밖에 없었다. 그리고 그때부터 스물한 살, 맹호부대에 입대할 때까지 해 뜰 때 발동이 걸렸다가 해 질 때 발동이 꺼지는 경운기처럼 뒷동산 감자밭에서부터 안목골 논까지 하루 종일 터덜터덜 걸어다니면서 일을 해야만 했다.

그런 삼촌을 서울로 떠밀어 올린 것은 할머니였다.

—갸가, 제대한 후에도 계속 농사만 지었는데, 아 어느 날 내가 갸 참을 가져다주려고 안목골 논까지 리어카를 끌고 갔거든……

—아이, 참, 할머니. 또 그 얘기 하려는구나. 아. 글쎄 그 얘긴 하지 말래도.

—아, 그러니까 잘 들어봐, 이놈아…… 그때 갸가 논두렁 한쪽에 이렇게 누워서 자고 있었는데 말이야, 내가 옆으로 가만히 다가가 내려다보니까, 아, 글쎄 추리닝 바지 아래로 갸 자지가, 갸 자지가 이렇게, 이렇게 서 있는 거야……

14

born, Grandfather died in an accident when he fell off the town bridge. Then Father and Second Uncle, who were respectively nine and seven years older than Uncle, both entered a trade school in Seoul and so Uncle was left with no choice but to finish junior high school and settle into rural life. From then until he was twenty-one and serving his mandatory military service in the Tiger Division, he was like a machine, starting his engine at dawn and shutting it off at dusk. From the potato fields of the back hill to the rice paddies in the inner valley, he plodded along and worked all day.

The person who forced Uncle to go to Seoul was Grandmother.

"Your uncle, even after getting discharged, all he did was work the farm. One day, I packed a pushcart with refreshments to take to your uncle in the rice paddies."

"Grandmother. Not again. I told you not to keep telling that story."

"Be quiet and just listen. Your uncle was lying down like this in the ridge between the rice paddies. I snuck up next to him and looked down and, my goodness, from inside his sweatpants, his thing, his penis, was sticking up like, like this—"

할머니는 그 이야기를 할 때마다 당신의 오른손을 잠옷바지 아래로 넣어 들썩거리곤 했다.

—아, 그걸 내가 처음 봤을 땐 어찌나 민망하고 놀랐던지…… 아, 근데 사람 마음이 또 요상한 게, 그걸 힐끔힐끔 내려다보고 있자니 이 할미 마음이 한편으론 짠해지는 거야…… 그래서 내 한참을 그 옆에 가만히 앉아 있다가 그냥 왔지 뭐냐.

할머니는 그길로 읍내 당숙에게 전화를 넣어 삼촌의 일자리를 부탁했다고 했다. 그게 82년 여름의 일이었다.

—나는 갸를 그렇게 서울로 올려 보내면 지 형들만큼은 아니더라도 그냥 저랑 어울리는 짝 만나 알콩달콩 잘 살 줄 알았지 뭐냐…… 한데, 이건 뭐 계절이 몇 번 바뀌도록 여자가 생겼는지 안 생겼는지 도통 알 수가 있어야지. 어쩌다 노는 날 집에 내려와도 아무 말 없이 장작이나 패다 가니…… 내가 두 해쯤 지나 네 고모를 일부러 같은 공장에 취직시켜 갸한테 올려 보낸 것도 다 그것 좀 알아보라고. 그것 좀 캐보라고 그런 거거든.

하지만, 당시 스무 살이었던 고모가 전해온 소식은 할머니를 충분히 실망시키고도 남는 것이었다. 고향에서

16

Whenever Grandmother told this story, she'd stick her right hand into her pajama pants and move it up and down.

"When I first saw it, I felt so shocked and embarrassed. But, y'know, what's really odd about a person's emotions is that while standing there, looking down at him, a part of me started to feel sorry for him. So I just stood there silently, then went back."

When Grandmother got back home, she immediately called up a relative and asked him to find Uncle a place to work. This was back in the summer of '82.

"Even if he couldn't live up to his older brothers, I thought that if I sent him up to Seoul he would at least find a nice girl and live happily. But, as the seasons changed, I couldn't tell if he was seeing someone or not. When he came down to visit on his days off, he didn't say a word and just chopped firewood. After the second year, I deliberately got your aunt a job at the same factory and sent her to Seoul. I wanted her to look into it, to find out what was going on."

Auntie, who was twenty at the time, only had devastating news to report back to Grandmother. Uncle was living exactly the same as when he'd

랑 똑같다고, 아침부터 한밤중 잔업이 끝날 때까지 말한마디 없이 기계에서 밀려나오는 원단만 받아낸다는 것, 어쩌다 휴일이 돌아와도 자취방에서 도통 나오지 않고 잠만 자거나 라디오만 듣는다는 것. 회사 여공들 사이에서도 '어머, 그런 사람이 있었어?'로 통한다는 것, 그러니, 자기부터 먼저 시집을 보내줘야 할 것 같다는 얘기……

—네, 그래서 그때부터 악착같이 저금을 했다는 거 아니냐. 네 고모한테 들으니까 그때 젊은것들은 자동차 있는 남자들을 좋아한다고 해서, 오냐, 그럼 내가 우리 막내 그놈 한 대 사주자, 그래서 처녀들을 한꺼번에 세 명, 네 명씩 태우고 돌아다니게 해주자, 나는 뭐 열 며느리 마다하지 않을 자신이 있었으니까…… 그래서 그때까지만 해도 네 애비에게도, 네 작은애비에게도 없던 자동차를 떡하니 사준 게지. 내가 갸한테 뭘 사준 건 그게 처음이었어……

할머니는 삼촌이 프라이드를 몰고 서울로 올라간 그 다음 주말부터 계속 다리 건너 신작로까지 나가 한나절을 앉아 있다가 돌아왔다고 했다. 옥니만 아니면 되는데, 옥니만 아니면 되는데…… 할머니는 그렇게 중얼

lived at home. From early morning until he finished working overtime, he didn't say a word and just collected the fabric that rolled out from the machines. When he got a rare day off, he didn't leave his room and either slept or listened to the radio. Among the female factory workers, all they said was, "Oh? We've never heard of him." And so Auntie told Grandmother that she'd probably end up getting married first.

"So from that day forward, I started saving up every penny I earned. I'd heard from your aunt that young girls back then liked men who had cars. So, ok, if that's the case, then I'd buy my youngest a car so he could cart around three, no, four girls at a time. Heck, I wouldn't have cared if he brought home ten wives. So that's why I bought it for him, a car that not even your father, not even your second uncle, ever had. It was the first time I'd ever bought him anything..."

Grandmother said that the weekend after Uncle left for Seoul in the Pride, she started going all the way out to the new highway across the bridge and would sit there waiting for almost half a day before returning. She'd sit there mumbling over and over, "No crooked teeth, no crooked teeth," and would

19

거리면서, 삼촌이 프라이드 조수석에 태우고 데려올 여자를 머릿속에 그리고 또 그려보았다고 했다.

하지만 할머니의 그런 바람과는 달리, 삼촌은 그 뒤로도, 한 달이 지나고 두 달이 지나고 일 년이 다 지나도록 처녀를 데리고 나타나진 않았다.

대신…… 삼촌은 프라이드와 사랑에 빠지게 되었다.

그러니까 이 글은 바로 그 사정에 대한 이야기이다. 나 역시도 한참 후에야 알게 된 삼촌과 프라이드의 사정 말이다.

2

내가 지금도 생생히 기억하는 삼촌은 항상 프라이드 운전석을 최대한 뒤로 젖힌 채, 그 위에 침낭을 깔고 자고 있는 모습이었다. 87년 추석 이후, 내가 삼촌의 얼굴을 본 것은 손으로 꼽을 수 있을 만큼 많지 않았는데, 그것은 대부분 설날 아침이거나 입춘 근처에 있는 할아버지 제삿날 저녁이었다. 가평 집 안방에 병풍이 쳐지고 지방이 세워질 때쯤이면, 항상 할머니가 부엌으로 따로

try to picture over and over what type of girl Uncle would bring in the passenger seat.

But contrary to her hopes, even after a month, two months, even a year, Uncle never came with a girl.

Instead, Uncle fell in love with...the Pride.

2

The image of Uncle that I can still clearly see is of him in the driver's seat of the Pride, seat tilted all the way back, asleep in a sleeping bag. After the *Chuseok* of '87, I could count with my fingers the number of times I'd seen him, and usually, it was either on the morning of New Year or Grandfather's anniversary, which was near the first day of spring. When the folding screen was put up in the living room and the ancestral tablet was set in place, Grandmother would always pull me into the kitchen and whisper quietly, "Open the front gate and go check the back hill near the poplar trees. If your uncle is there, tell him to hurry up and come in."

Uncle came on some New Year mornings and didn't show up on others. On the days he came I'd find the Pride and its entire windshield covered in

나를 불러내어 작은 목소리로 말하곤 했다.

　—대문 열고 저기 저 뒷동산 밭 미루나무 아래 가봐
라. 삼촌 왔으면 어여 들어오라고 하고.

　삼촌은 어느 해 설날엔 왔고, 또 어느 해 설날엔 오지
않았다. 프라이드 창문 전체를 뒤덮은 하얀 서리를 부
챗살 모양으로 긁어내보면, 거기 삼촌이 히터도 켜지
않은 채 잠들어 있었다. 뒷좌석 한편엔 휴대용 가스버
너와 코펠, 커다란 플라스틱 물통이 하나 놓여 있었고,
운동화와 흙이 잔뜩 묻은 안전화, 공구들이 가득 담긴
쌀자루도 눈에 들어왔다. 삼촌은 자리에서 일어나면 항
상 자동차 시동을 먼저 걸었는데, 그런 다음에야 눈곱
을 떼고 기지개를 펴고 운전석 문을 열고 나와 내 머리
를 한번 쓰다듬어주었다. 그리고 5분 정도 보닛 바로 옆
에 쭈그리고 앉아 담배를 한 대 다 피운 후, 다시 시동을
끄고 그제야 집으로 들어가곤 했다.

　내 기억이 정확하다면, 삼촌은 프라이드를 타기 시작
한 지 두 달 만에 다니던 공장을 그만두고 전국을 떠돌
기 시작했다. 주로 물막이 현장이나 신축 아파트 공사
장들을 떠돌아다니며 간간이 일을 하는 모양이었는데,
따로 방을 잡거나 살림을 차린 눈치는 아니었다. 차례

frost. When I scraped a fan-shaped portion of it away, I'd always see Uncle sleeping inside without even the heater turned on. I could see a portable gas burner and a camping pot in the backseat, a huge plastic bottle of water, mud-caked sneakers and safety boots, and a rice sack that was packed full with tools. The first thing he'd do when he woke up was start the engine. Then he'd wipe the gunk out of his eyes, stretch his arms way out to the sides, open the driver's side door, step out, and muss my hair. Then, for about the next five minutes, he'd crouch beside the hood of the car and smoke a cigarette down to a tiny burning nub before turning off the engine and going inside.

If my memory serves me correctly, after two months of driving the Pride, Uncle left his job at the factory and started wandering all over the country. It seemed like he was moving around clapboard building sites or apartment construction sites to stay afloat, but it didn't seem like he'd gotten a place or had set up house somewhere. When the holiday ancestral rites or anniversary rites finished, Father, looking irritated, would make all of us kids leave the room. Then the yelling would start. Usually, it was Father or Second Uncle's

나 제사가 어느 정도 마무리되고 나면, 아버지는 짜증난 듯한 표정으로 나와 사촌동생들을 모두 방 밖으로 내보내곤 했다. 그리고 그 뒤엔 항상 큰소리가 튀어나왔다. 주로 정신 좀 차리라는, 언제까지 그렇게 살 거냐는, 아버지와 작은아버지의 목소리였다. 어느 해엔 누군가 손찌검하는 소리가 부엌까지 들려오기도 했는데, 그때마다 할머니는 괜스레 어머니와 작은어머니에게 손이 굼뜨다는 둥, 아직까지 시어미가 들기름이 어디 있는지 일일이 가르쳐주어야 하겠냐며 신경질을 냈다.

삼촌은 차례나 제사가 끝난 후, 대개 한두 시간도 지나지 않아 사라졌다. 화장실을 가는가 싶었는데, 마당에 나가보면 어느새 멀리, 동네 초입을 빠져나가고 있는 프리이드의 붉은색 후미등이 눈에 들어왔다. 그렇게 작게 작게 사라져가는 후미등을 한참 동안 바라보고 있자면 왠지 모르게 쓸쓸하고 외로운 마음이 들기도 했는데, 사실 그런 감정은 잠시였고, 나는 나도 모르게 휴우, 긴 한숨을 내뱉곤 했다. 어쨌든 삼촌 때문에 집안 분위기가 엉망이 되는 것은 사실이었으니까. 마치 그때부터 다시 명절이 시작되는 듯한 느낌이 들기도 했다.

93년도 설이던가, 한번은 사촌 여동생이 삼촌의 점퍼

24

voice: "Get your act together! When are you going to stop living like this?" One year, the sound of someone getting slapped could be heard all the way to the kitchen. Whenever this happened, Grandmother would snap at Mother and Second Aunt for no reason, telling them that they were working too slow, and asking them why their mother-in-law still had to tell them where the perilla oil was stored.

When the holiday ancestral rites or anniversary rites finished, Uncle never stayed around longer than a couple of hours. If I thought he was going to the bathroom, I'd go out to the yard and see the red tailgates of the Pride already far away, passing through the entrance of the town. Standing there, watching the tailgates grow tinier and tinier, I'd somehow get a feeling of isolation and loneliness, but only for a brief moment before letting out a long, perfunctory sigh. Whatever the case, it was true that Uncle's presence made a mess of our family's atmosphere. Only after he left would it feel like the real holidays could begin.

One time on New Year, in '93 I think, my younger cousin pilfered the car keys from Uncle's jacket and snuck into the Pride. Turned out she wanted to lis-

에서 몰래 차 키를 빼내 프라이드에 숨어든 적이 있었다. 제 딴에는 집에서 가져온 카세트테이프를 듣고 싶어서 그랬던 모양인데, 시동도 제대로 걸지 않은 상태에서 히터와 오디오를 켜고 있는 바람에 그만 배터리가 모두 방전되고 말았다. 뒤늦게 그 사실을 안 삼촌은, 그때부터 다음 날 아침 서비스센터 직원이 트럭을 몰고 직접 찾아올 때까지 단 한 발짝도 프라이드 옆을 떠나지 않았다. 밤이 늦도록 집으로 들어오지 않는 삼촌을 보다 못한 작은어머니가 몇 번 대문 밖으로 나가봤지만, 번번이 혼자 돌아오곤 했다.

　—뭐래, 안 들어오겠대?

　작은아버지가 묻자, 작은어머니는 말없이 고개만 끄덕거렸다.

　—한데…… 한데, 삼촌이 좀 이상해요.

　—뭐가?

　—차를…… 차 앞머리를…… 이렇게 꽉 끌어안고 있어요…… 마치 애인이라도 되는 것처럼.

　그 말을 들은 아버지는 허, 참, 하며 고개를 절레절레 흔들었고, 할머니는 슬그머니 자리에서 일어나 방 밖으로 나가버렸다. 언젠가 내가 그날 일을 병실에 누워 있

ten to the cassette tape that she'd brought from home. But because she had the heater and radio running without properly turning the key, the battery ended up completely draining. After discovering this too late, Uncle didn't take a single step away from the Pride until the tow truck from the service center came the next morning. Unable to watch Uncle stand outside in the dark any longer, Second Aunt had gone out to him several times but each time, she had come back alone.

"What did he say? He's not coming in?"

Second Aunt said nothing and just shook her head.

"But, but. Uncle is acting a bit strange."

"How so?"

"The car...the hood of the car...he's lying there hugging it...as if it were his lover or something."

Hearing this, Father scoffed and shook his head. Grandmother quietly got up and left the room.

Sometime later, when Grandmother was lying in her hospital bed, I asked her about that night. She also remembered the events of that night very clearly. She'd gone out a couple of times to check on him.

"Your uncle...he's a sentimental soul. You know

는 할머니에게 물어본 적이 있었는데, 할머니 역시 그때 일을 또렷하게 기억하고 있었다. 할머니 또한 그날 밤 종종 삼촌이 있는 곳으로 나가봤던 것이다.

—갸가…… 속정이 깊어서…… 그게 누렁이 팔아서 장만한 거잖냐? 그저 그게 누렁이다, 생각해서 그런 게지. 내가 그날 갸들 둘한테 담요 덮어주고 왔어.

할머니는 그렇게 이해했을지 몰라도, 그러나 가족들 중 그 누구도 그런 삼촌을 이해한 사람은, 아니 이해하려고 노력한 사람은 없었다. 그저 삼촌에게서 무언가가 살짝, 빠져나갔다고만 생각했을 뿐, 다른 것은 없었다. 그도 그럴 것이 삼촌은 그 뒤로도 20년 가까운 세월을 계속 프라이드에서 나오지 않았으니까…… 길을 가던 도중 어쩌다 불쑥 하얀색 프라이드를 마주치기라도 하면 무의식중에 꾸벅, 고개를 숙이고 싶은 마음이 들었던 건 비단 나뿐만은 아니었던지, 지금은 호주에 가서 살고 있는 사촌 여동생은 언젠가 한번 횡단보도 앞에서 하얀색 프라이드와 마주쳤을 때, 저도 모르게 속엣말로 '숙모님'이라고 불러봤다고 고백했을 정도이니, 말 다한 것이다.

we sold Nureongi to buy that car, right? So to him, that car was Nureongi. That night, I went out and tucked them both in with a blanket."

Grandmother might have understood Uncle, but no one else in the family did or, rather, no one even wanted to try. They just thought that there was something slightly off, something not quite right with him. That was all. And this was justified since, for about twenty years after that night, Uncle remained inside the Pride. After that, whenever I walked down the street and saw a white Pride pass by, I'd automatically feel the urge to bow. And it wasn't just me. My younger cousin who now lives in Australia confessed that one time, when she was standing at a crosswalk, she saw a white Pride pass by and, without thinking, she'd whispered, "Aunt." So what else was there left to say?

3

It was six years ago in spring, the exact date being April 6, 2004 (I found out the exact date much later on), when Uncle disappeared after parking the Pride next to the wall in front of our house at dawn. Father, who'd gone out to the front gate to

3

그런 삼촌이 우리 집 담벼락 옆에 프라이드를 주차해 놓고 사라진 것은 6년 전 어느 봄날, 그러니까 정확하게 말하자면 2004년 4월 6일(정확한 날짜는 나 또한 훨씬 후에 알게 된 것이었다), 새벽의 일이었다. 아침에 신문을 가지러 대문 앞까지 나간 아버지는 우유 투입구에서 낯선 자동차 키를 발견했고, 곧이어 아버지의 소나타 뒤에 얌전히 주차되어 있던 삼촌의 프라이드를 보게 되었다. 삼촌은 타고 있지 않았다.

하필 그날 나는 같은 대학원에 다니고 있던 사람들과 왜 우리가 결혼정보회사 듀오에 가입될 수 없는가에 대해 밤새 진지하고 심도 있는 토론을, 다량의 음주와 함께 나눈 후 첫차를 타고 돌아오는 길이었기에, 골목길에서 아버지와 마주치자마자 움찔, 그 자리에 굳은 듯 멈춰 설 수밖에 없었다. 또 한 소리 제대로 듣겠구나, 각오하고 있었는데, 뜻밖에도 아버지는 계속 주차된 프라이드만 이리저리 살필 뿐, 내겐 별 관심을 보이지 않았다.

―이게 네 삼촌 차 맞지?

get the newspaper, found a strange key deposited in the milk delivery slot and then saw Uncle's Pride parked quietly behind his Sonata. Uncle wasn't inside.

Out of all the days that Uncle could've left his car behind, he'd left it on the same day I'd taken the first train home after a long night of heavy drinking with my fellow grad school classmates. We'd stayed up all night having a serious and deep discussion about why we weren't suitable candidates to sign up with the marriage consulting agency, Duo. Arriving on the scene, I immediately froze on the spot. I braced myself for an earful, but on the contrary, Father didn't say a word and just carefully examined the parked Pride.

"That's your uncle's car, right?"

That's when I turned and saw the Pride. Just by looking at it, I knew it was Uncle's car. The license plate was exactly the same, as were the aluminum spokes on the wheel. It was Uncle's longtime lover. As if the Pride had just been washed, there wasn't a speck of dust on it and it glistened under the freshly risen sun. Uncle had driven the car for nearly twenty years but, apart from the color fading slightly to a pearl white, the bumper didn't even

그제야 나도 주차되어 있던 프라이드로 눈길을 돌리게 되었다. 그건 한눈에 봐도 삼촌의 차가 틀림없었다. 번호판도 예전 그대로였고, 사선으로 된 알루미늄 휠도 변함없는, 삼촌의 오래된 연인이 맞았다. 프라이드는 이제 막 세차를 끝낸 듯 먼지 하나 없이, 그때 막 떠오르던 해에 반사돼 번들거리고 있었다. 20년 가까이 운행된 자동차였지만, 색깔만 조금 진주색에 가깝게 바랬을 뿐, 범퍼엔 잔 흠집 하나 나 있지 않았다.

　—한데, 이걸 왜 집에 던져놓고…… 어딜 간 거야?

　아버지는 손에 들고 있던 자동차 키를 흔들며 계속 고개를 갸웃거렸다. 그땐 할머니가 우리 집에서 함께 산 지도 벌써 8년 가까이 흐른 뒤인지라, 나는 당연히 삼촌이 할머니를 만나러 온 것이라고 생각했다. 그래서 아마 목욕탕에 간 거 같다고, 그래야 삼촌도 듀오에 가입할 수 있지 않겠냐며, 횡설수설 아버지에게 말을 늘어놓았던 것 같다. 그러니까 그때까지만 해도 나는, 삼촌이 하루가 지나고 이틀이 지나고 우리 동네 목욕탕들이 죄다 찜질방으로 상호를 바꿀 때까지 돌아오지 않을 줄은 상상도 하지 못한 것이다. 상상은 무슨 상상, 그저 빨리 눕고만 싶었을 뿐이었다.

have a single scratch on it.

"But...why'd he leave it here?" I mumbled. "Where'd he go?"

Father dangled Uncle's key and kept cocking his head from side to side. Grandmother had been living with us for eight years then, so, naturally, I thought that Uncle had come to see her. I think I began to ramble on about how Uncle had probably gone to a bathhouse and, that if he had, then he'd also be able to sign up with Duo. There was no way I could've imagined that after a day, after two, after all the neighborhood bathhouses changed their signs to *jjimjilbang*, Uncle would still not have returned. Imagine? Forget imagine. All I could think about then was my bed.

4

Kia Motors began production of the Pride in March of '87. It was the first hatchback in Korea. It had a 4-cylinder engine and it came in two models: a 1139cc-70 horsepower model and a 1323cc-78 horsepower one. After seeing the new hatchback style for the first time, people who were only used to seeing sedans with their big trunks pro-

4

프라이드는 87년 3월부터 기아자동차에서 생산되기 시작한, 우리나라 최초의 해치백 스타일의 자동차였다. 엔진은 직렬 4기통 1139시시 70마력짜리와, 1323시시 78마력 가솔린 엔진 두 가지 모델이 있었다. 그때까지만 해도 트렁크가 뒤로 삐죽 튀어나와 있는 세단 모델에 익숙해 있던 사람들은, 처음 보는 해치백 스타일의 자동차를 두고 이런저런 말들이 많았다. 뒤에서 차가 받으면 운전자가 즉사한다는 둥, 트렁크엔 도시락 하나 실을 수 없을 거라는 둥, 기름통이 너무 작아 오토바이랑 다를 바 없을 거라는 둥, 앞에 손잡이만 하나 달면 딱 리어카라는 둥, 대부분 무시와 비하의 말들이 주를 이뤘다. 하지만 그해 3월 5일 서울 영동 무공종합전시장에서 열린 신차 발표회장엔 나흘 동안 무려 18만 명의 시민들이 한꺼번에 몰려, 그런 말들을 모두 무색하게 만들었다. 신차 발표회 후 한 달 만에 가계약 건수가 9천 대를 넘어섰고, 87년이 다 지나가기 전까지 그해 계획했던 총 3만 대의 판매 실적을 모두 달성해, 당시로서는 어마어마한 성공을 거두기도 했다. 프라이드가 그토

truding out their backs had a lot to say. Most of the talk was belittling and derogatory such as,

"You'll die on impact if you get rear-ended."

"A lunch box won't even fit in the trunk."

"The oil tank's so small it's basically the same as a motorcycle."

"Put handles on the front and you'll have yourself a pushcart."

But at the official car launch held that year on March 5 at the Yeongdong Exhibition Center, as many as 18,000 citizens were in attendance and all their comments were put to rest. Within a month after the car was launched, pre-sale contracts reached over 9,000 and before the year was over, they'd far exceeded their initial target expectations by selling more than 30,000 units that year. The reason why the Pride became so popular in such a short period of time was its affordable price and its unmatchable fuel efficiency.

But you also couldn't ignore the power of its intensive ad campaign that began broadcasting that May. The ad featured a young man and woman dressed casually in white, walking along the Han River before getting into the Pride and driving across the city and into the sunset. The slogan

록 단기간 안에 인기를 끌 수 있었던 비결은 저렴한 차량 가격과 다른 차들과는 비교할 수 없을 만큼 좋은 연비가 톡톡히 한몫했지만, 그해 3월부터 집중적으로 방영된 텔레비전 CF의 공 또한 무시할 순 없을 것이다. 하얀색 캐주얼 차림의 젊은 두 남녀가 한강변을 걸어가다가 프라이드를 타고 석양이 지는 도시 저쪽으로 사라지는 광고는, '도시의 젊은 생활, 나의 삶 나의 꿈, 프라이드'라는 카피와 함께 매시간 텔레비전에서 흘러나왔다. 지금 생각해보면 조금 유치하기까지 한 그 광고는, 남자 모델의 특이한 승차 자세 때문에 더 큰 화제를 몰고 왔다. 남자 모델은 한쪽 다리를 미리 쭉 펴서, 그러니까 마치 태권도의 뒷발차기 비슷한 자세로 몸을 낮춰 운전석에 올라탔는데(아마도 차체가 낮아서 그랬던 모양이었다), 그 모습이 사람들에겐 낯설고 또 한편으론 신기하게 여겨진 모양이었다. 그 광고가 나온 이후, 거리 곳곳에서 택시를 그런 자세로 올라타는 사람들을 종종 발견할 수 있었고, 나와 내 친구들은 자주 그런 자세로 버스에 올라타다가 기사 아저씨에게 호되게 욕을 얻어먹기도 했다.

프라이드는 이후 몇 차례 보디 형식을 추가해 모델

was, "Carefree city life, my life, my dream, Pride."
Now that I think about it, it was a pretty cheesy ad,
but it gained more and more attention because of
the way the male model entered the car, stretching
out one of his legs as if he was doing a Taekwon-
do sidekick, and lowering himself into the driver's
seat (probably because the car was so low). It seemed
like people found the image strange but were also
fascinated by it. After the ad was aired you could
see people everywhere getting into cabs like that;
my friends and I even got yelled at by a bus driver
when we tried to board the bus like that.

Over the years, the Pride added a series of different models to their lineup with variations on the
car body and then in January of 2000, it stopped
production. It had sold a total of somewhere near
70,000 units and combined with the units that were
exported by Ford and Mazda in the form of OEM,
Kia had manufactured over 100,000 units. I once
read a car specialist's review that "ultimately, the car
was a failure." The gist of his argument was that
"cars should have a certain level of defects, certain
causes that would require after-sales service. But
the Pride didn't have any of these. When looked at
from a profit-based point of view, it was a car that

라인업을 늘려나가다가, 2000년 1월 최종 단종되고 말았다. 그때까지 총 판매 대수는 70만 대가 조금 넘었고, 포드 자동차와 마쓰다 자동차에 OEM 방식으로 수출된 물량까지 합치면 총 100만 대가 넘게 생산되었다. 예전 어느 자동차 전문기자가 프라이드에 대해서 '결과적으로 실패한 모델'이라고 쓴 글을 읽은 적이 있었는데, 요지는 대충 이런 것이었다. '자동차는 어느 정도 결함도 있고, AS 유발 효과라는 것도 있어야 하는 법인데, 프라이드는 그런 게 없었다. 수익적 차원에서 보면 회사에 아무런 보탬도 되지 않았던 자동차였다.' 프라이드에 대해 욕을 하는 글인지 칭찬하는 글인지 도통 알 수는 없으나, 그의 평가와 일반인들의 평가는 크게 다르지 않았다. 어떤 사람은 프라이드의 출시로 인해 바야흐로 우리나라에 1가구 1차 시대가 열렸다고 평하기도 했으니까. 물론 다 지난 다음에, 프라이드가 단종된 이후에야 나온 말들이지만 말이다.

5

2004년 4월이면 내가 운전면허를 딴 지 채 6개월도

just didn't make enough money for the manufac-
turer." I wasn't sure if he was trying to criticize the
car or commend it, but his opinion and the opin-
ions of the people who'd bought the car were basically the same. Some people even said that with
the launch of the Pride, Korea entered the one car
per household era. Of course, all these comments
were made later on, after the Pride was discontin-
ued.

5

May of 2004 wasn't even six months after I'd gotten my license, so whenever I saw a bathroom
sink, I felt the urge to turn it like a steering wheel
and while sitting on the bus, I'd flex my right foot
and gently press my foot to the air. It was around
that time when, leaping at the chance to drive my
father's Sonata, I ended up having to replace the
left side mirror and entire rear bumper. It was also
around the time when I stayed up all night on the
Internet, looking up used Matiz prices, then
searched for part-time teaching positions at cram
schools, then went back to looking up interest
rates on monthly payments for an Avante. If you

지나지 않았던 때인지라, 세숫대야만 봐도 무작정 이리저리 돌려보고 싶은 마음이 생기고, 버스 좌석에 앉아도 오른쪽 발바닥을 살짝 세워 허공을 지그시 밟아대던, 그런 시절이었다. 호시탐탐 아버지의 소나타를 노리다가 좌측 사이드 미러와 뒷범퍼를 전부 교체하게 만들었던 것도 그맘때였고, 인터넷으로 밤새 중고 마티즈 시세를 알아보다가 다시 학원 파트타이머 강사 자리를 알아보다가, 또다시 아반떼의 할부 금리를 알아보던 시절이기도 했다. 차가 꼭 필요한 이유를 대라면 당연 아무런 말도 할 수 없었지만, 아무런 이유 없이 차를 몰고 다니는 친구들은 주위에 넘치고 넘쳐났기에, 나는 종종 까닭 없이 불행하다는 생각에 빠지기도 했다. 자동차 회사들 또한 아무런 이유 없이 차를 모는 사람들을 주 고객 대상으로 삼아 '제로백'이니 '코너링'이니 하는 것들을 주요 선전문구로 내세웠으니, 거참, 사람 멍하게 만드는 것도 한순간의 일이었다. 아무런 문제도 없고, 아무런 불편도 없는 상태에서 느끼는 불행이란, 곧잘 우울증으로 이어질 수 있다는 것을 깨닫게 된 것도 아마 그즈음의 일이었을 것이다.

asked me why I absolutely needed a car, I had nothing to say. But because I was surrounded by an overwhelming number of people my age that had cars for no reason, I sometimes felt like I was miserable, for no reason at all. And because the car dealerships were targeting people like me as their main clientele, and came up with ad slogans that included terms like "0-100km" and "Cornering," well, I didn't stand a chance. It was around that time that I realized the misery you feel when nothing is wrong, when there's no cause for complain, can lead you to depression.

It was during this period that Uncle's car key sat quietly on top of our shoe rack for over a week. In the beginning, I had no intention of laying a finger on it. This was because it was his car, Uncle's car. To Uncle, the Pride was like his lover. I thought that to secretly take the Pride out for a spin would be almost blasphemous, but in truth, my fear was much greater. I felt that if I came back home after taking a ride in it, I'd return to find Uncle standing there, feet planted in the middle of the road, waiting for me. So even if I was stuck grabbing bathroom sinks and turning them like steering wheels, I wouldn't turn human courtesy, not even the circu-

그런 시절에, 삼촌의 자동차 키가 일주일 넘게 우리 집 신발장 위에 얌전히 놓여 있었다⋯⋯ 처음엔 정말 이지 손톱만큼도 그것을 건드릴 생각은 하지 못했다. 다른 사람도 아닌, 삼촌의 자동차였기 때문이었다. 삼촌에겐 애인과도 같은 프라이드였다. 그런 프라이드를 몰래 탄다는 건⋯⋯ 그 자체가 불경스럽게 여겨지기도 했지만, 사실은 두려운 마음이 더 컸다. 차를 끌고 나갔 다가 집으로 돌아와보면, 삼촌이 그 자리 그대로 우뚝 서서, 나를 기다리고 있을 것만 같았다. 그러니까 아무 리 세숫대야를 잡고 이리저리 돌려대는 처지라 해도, 사람에 대한 예의까지는, '예의'라는 단어의 초성까지는, 자동차 핸들로 보지 않았던 것이다.

　하지만, 삼촌이 일주일이 지나 열흘이 넘도록 연락 한 번 없이 돌아오지 않자, 슬금슬금 내 안에서 다른 가정 들이 자라나기 시작했다. 일테면, 삼촌이 차를 바꾼 게 아닐까, 하는 가정, 혹은 삼촌이 이라크나 두바이로 일 자리를 찾아 떠났을지 모른다는 가정, 그것도 아니면 삼촌이 음주운전으로 면허가 취소되었을지 모른다는 가정, 그것도 아니라면⋯⋯ 그냥 불현듯 내가 생각나 서, 네가 할머니 때문에 고생이 많구나, 하면서 선물로

lar shapes in the word "courtesy," into a steering wheel.

However, for over a week and even after more than ten days had passed, Uncle never called and didn't come back.

Little by little, probing thoughts began to grow within me. For instance, maybe Uncle had bought a new car, or maybe he'd left for Iraq or Dubai in search of work. Or, if not that, then maybe his driver's license had been revoked after a DUI. And if it wasn't for any of these reasons, then perhaps he'd suddenly thought of me, of rewarding me for listening to Grandmother all day long since Uncle probably had to sit through Grandmother's stories as well when he was younger.

After two weeks of torturously battling with these speculations, on the Friday of the last week of April, I finally snuck out the front door clutching Uncle's car key. I had concluded that if I didn't at least start the car, if I continued to neglect the Pride, it would be a discourtesy to the car. Uncle would understand my deeper intentions. Hey, at least I was a youth who wasn't lacking when it came to courtesy.

When I turned the ignition of Uncle's Pride for

주고 갔을 가정…… 삼촌 역시 젊은 시절 할머니 이야기를 듣느라 고생깨나 했을 게 분명하니까……

결국 그런 가정과 가정의 지난한 싸움 끝에, 내가 삼촌의 자동차 키를 손아귀에 감싸 쥔 채 조용히 현관문 밖으로 나선 것은 그로부터 다시 보름이 지난, 4월의 마지막 주 금요일의 일이었다. 어쨌든 너무 오랫동안 시동을 걸지 않고 방치하면, 그것 또한 차에 대한 예의가 아니라는 것이, 삼촌도 그런 내 마음을 이해해주리라는 것이, 나의 최종 결론이었다. 하여간, 예의 하나는 어디에 내놔도 빠지지 않았던 청춘이었던 것이다.

삼촌의 프라이드에 처음 시동을 걸었을 때, 그때 들었던 엔진 소리를 지금도 잊을 수가 없다. 이미 햇수로 꼬박 18년이 되었고, 계기판에 나와 있는 주행거리는 47만 킬로미터를 넘어서고 있었지만, 프라이드의 엔진은 부드럽고 조용하게, 마치 난로 위 주전자처럼 천천히, 그리고 단호하게 움직이기 시작했다. 기름은 가득 채워져 있었고, 사이드브레이크는 단단히 잠긴 상태였다. 실내엔 희미하게 알코올 냄새 같은 것이 배어 있었는

the first time, the sound of the engine I heard in that moment became something I still can't forget. The car was already eighteen years old and the odometer read upwards of 470,000km, but the engine purred smoothly and quietly. Slowly and determinedly, like a kettle beginning to boil on top of a wood stove, the Pride began to come alive. The gas tank was full and the parking brake was set tight. The faint smell of alcohol permeated the interior, but it resembled the unique, new car smell that I'd smelled before in Father's car. The seats were clean and Uncle's junk, which I'd seen in the car before, was nowhere in sight. The rubber floor mat of the driver's side was worn out and the edges were cracked, but the one on the passenger's side was clean as if it had just been dipped in water.

With the engine still running, I took my sweet time looking around and scanning the interior. Then, I permitted myself a single hand on the steering wheel. It had been broken in well so it wasn't too stiff or too loose. As I held the steering wheel, I exhaled deeply. Out of all my wandering notions and hypotheses, one thing had become clear. For whatever reason, Uncle had parted with

데, 그건 일전에 아버지 차에서 맡아보았던 새 차 특유의 냄새를 닮아 있기도 했다. 시트도 깨끗했고, 예전 내가 보았던 삼촌의 자질구레한 짐들 역시 하나 보이지 않았다. 검은 고무재질로 만든 발판은, 운전석 쪽은 닳고 닳아 끝 부분이 모두 갈라져 있었지만, 조수석 쪽은 이제 막 물에 담갔다가 뺀 듯 말끔했다.

나는 시동을 건 채, 한참 동안 차 내부를 두리번거리면서 살펴보았다. 그리고 핸들을 살짝 잡아보았다. 핸들은 길이 잘 든 듯 너무 뻑뻑하지도, 또 너무 헐겁지도 않았다. 나는 핸들을 잡은 상태에서 숨을 한 번 길게 내쉬었다. 여러 가지 가정 중 하나의 가정은 확실해진 것 같았다. 왜인지는 알 수 없으나, 삼촌은 이제 이 프라이드와 영영 이별을 해버린 것만 같았다. 그냥 나도 모르게 그 순간, 그런 느낌이 들었다. 그렇다면…… 나는 브레이크 페달에서 발을 떼, 액셀 페달 위에 올려놓았다. 차는 아무 이상 없이 천천히 앞으로 움직이기 시작했다. 차가 서서히 움직이자, 나는 삼촌에 대한 생각은 자연스럽게 잊어버리고 말았다. 아직 초보 딱지를 떼지 못한 처지여서 그랬기도 했지만, 어쩌면 그것은 자연스러운 관성 같은 것이었는지도 몰랐다. 가정을 진실로

the Pride for good. I couldn't explain why, but in that moment, that's how I felt. I took my foot off the brake and placed it on the accelerator. Slowly and smoothly, the car began to move forward. As the car began to accelerate, I automatically stopped thinking about Uncle. This was probably because I was still a new driver, but perhaps it was like a type of natural inertia. The type of inertia that turns supposition into truth.

However, this rationalized state didn't last for long. That night, I found out that Uncle's Pride had one defect.

Uncle's Pride, Uncle's Pride…couldn't go in reverse.

6

The momentous discovery took place in the parking lot of Han River Park, at the section you can see from the Gayang Bridge. It would've been okay if I had been alone, but why is it that whenever new drivers grab steering wheels they feel like they're obligated to have someone else in the passenger seat? Like all new drivers, as soon as I'd taken control of the Pride and cleared the alley in

만들어버리는 관성 같은 것.

하지만, 그런 상태는 그리 오래가지는 못했는데, 그날 밤, 나는 삼촌의 프라이드의 어떤 결함에 대해서 곧장 알아버렸기 때문이었다.

삼촌의 프라이드는, 삼촌의 프라이드는…… 후진이 되질 않았다.

6

삼촌의 프라이드가 후진이 안 된다는 것을 내가 처음 알게 된 건 가양대교가 눈앞에 보이는 한강시민공원 주차장에서였다. 혼자였으면 차라리 좋았을 걸…… 왜 초보들은 운전대를 잡기만 하면 꼭 조수석에 누군가를 태워야 한다는 의무감에 휩싸이는지, 나 역시도 그날 프라이드를 몰고 집 앞 골목길을 빠져나오자마자 자연스럽게 한 여자아이부터 떠올렸고, 그래서 곧장 강변북로로 접어들고 말았다. 학교 신문사 간사 일을 하면서 알게 된 여자 후배였는데, 딱 한 번 단둘이 술자리를 가

front of my house, I automatically began to think of this one girl and I automatically found myself on the Gangbyeon Expressway. She was a junior I'd met while working as an assistant administrator at our college newspaper. We'd drank together just once but had gotten hammered and ended up sleeping together. But it's not like we ended up dating each other after. Sure, I'll admit that I was interested in her, but it didn't really seem like she felt the same way. She'd slapped me heartily on the shoulder and said, "Come on, that wasn't two people sleeping together. That was the alcohol sleeping together." There was nothing else I could do but return the slap to her shoulder and mumble, "Exactly. Why did we mix our alcohol last night?"

So when I showed up at her house in Ilsan that night and she said, "Wow, what's with the piece of junk?" I could only answer, "I know, right? My uncle asked me to take care of it for a bit. Do you want to go to Han River Park and get some fresh air?" In truth, I felt like we had missed out on something and I wanted to check if that something was still there.

But that night, before I could find out how she felt about me, I found out what was wrong with the

졌다가 엉망으로 취해 잠자리까지 하게 된 사이였다. 그렇다고 그 뒤 정식으로 사귀게 된 것은 또 아니었는데, 나야 어느 정도 호감을 갖고 있었다고 해도, 여자 후배의 입장은 꼭 그렇지만은 않은 것 같았기 때문이었다. 에이, 그거야 어디 사람끼리 잔 건가, 술끼리 서로 잔 거지. 여자 후배는 서슴없이 그런 말을 하면서 내 어깨를 퉁, 치기도 했다. 그러니, 나 역시도 별수 없이 퉁, 여자 후배의 어깨를 치며 그러게, 왜 술을 섞어 마시냐, 라고 웅얼거릴 수밖에.

그러니까 내가 그날 일산에 있는 그녀의 집을 찾아가 '어머, 이게 웬 똥차예요?'라는 소리를 듣고도 아무렇지 않게 '글쎄 말이야, 귀찮게 삼촌이 잠깐 맡아달라고 해서…… 한강에 바람이나 쐬러 갈까?' 운운했던 것은, 실은 무언가 아쉬운 마음이 남아서, 더 확인해보고 싶은 마음이 남아 있었기 때문이었다.

하지만. 그날 나는 그녀의 마음을 확인하기도 전에, 프라이드의 문제를 먼저 확인하게 되었고, 그것 때문에 그녀의 속내 따위는 전혀 생각하지도 못한 채, 낑낑, 계속 애꿎은 기어만 앞으로 뒤로 옮기다가, 결국 쓸쓸히

Pride first. I forgot about her completely and kept harassing the faultless gear, shifting it back and forth. In the end, I returned home feeling utterly empty. There was no other problem with the car. Just the one. When I put the gear in "R" and pressed the accelerator over and over again, the Pride just made loud revving noises but didn't move an inch. That was all. Of course if that had happened now, I would've put the car in neutral, leapt out of car to calculate the space and distance between it and the parking stall, pushed it from its trunk with two hands using an appropriate measure of strength, and then swiftly parked the car. But back then, the only experience I'd had driving was the three times I'd stolen my father's Sonata in the dead of night, and two out of those three times, I'd left an indelible scar on a telephone pole and a wall. All I knew was how to go forward and backwards but since I couldn't go backwards, of course I panicked. And since I panicked, I became more obsessed. If I couldn't park, then I could've avoided the situation by simply going for a drive around the area, but I couldn't think straight at the time. I just pulled and released the parking brake, turned the engine off and on, and shifted the gear over and

집으로 돌아오고 말았다. 다른 문제는 전혀 없었다. 오직 단 하나, 기어를 'R'에 놓고 아무리 액셀 페달을 밟아도, 밟고 또 밟아도, 프라이드는 요란한 소음만 낼 뿐, 꿈쩍도 하지 않았다는 것, 그게 전부였다. 지금이야 물론 그럴 경우, 기어를 중립에 놓고 재빠르게 운전석 밖으로 나가 차가 들어갈 공간을 나름 머릿속에 그리며 적절한 세기로 차 트렁크를 두 손으로 밀어 신속하게 주차를 끝냈겠지만, 그때야…… 더구나 당시 나는 운전 경력이라곤 고작 아버지의 소나타를 야밤에 세 번 훔쳐 몰아본 게 전부인, 그 세 번 중 두 번은 전봇대와 담벼락에 각각 씻을 수 없는 상처를 남긴, 말 그대로 전진과 후진만 아는 운전자였다. 한데, 그중 후진이 안 되는 경우이니…… 나는 당황하지 않을 수가 없었다. 그리고 당황해서, 더 집착하게 되었다. 주차가 제대로 안되면 대강 천천히 그 일대를 드라이브하면서 상황을 모면할 수도 있었을 텐데, 그러나 그때는 생각이 미처 거기까진 닿지 못했다. 그저, 계속 사이드브레이크를 당겼다가 풀었다가, 시동을 껐다가 켰다가, 기어를 'R'에서 다시 'D'로, 'D'에서 다시 'N'으로, 옮기고 옮겼을 뿐이었다. 그러는 사이 여자 후배는 조수석 문을 열고 나가 혼

over again from "R" to "D" and from "D" to "N."
While I was doing that, the junior opened the car
door, got out, and started walking along the riverside by herself. Even though I saw her, I just sat in
the Pride and turned the steering wheel back and
forth while wondering if something might be stuck
under the wheel.

She walked around the riverside by herself, went
to the snack bar and drank a soda, then came back.
Seeing me still in the driver's seat fumbling with the
gear, she gave me another hearty slap on the
shoulder and said, "And here I thought that only the
car was a piece of junk, but I see you're just the
same. I'm done, let's go."

7

This is also something that occurred to me in
hindsight, but if Uncle's Pride hadn't had any problems, if it had gone in reverse as smoothly and ef-
fortlessly as it had gone in forward drive, if, like
other cars, it had run as evenly as the melody of
"Für Elise," then would I have been able to drive
the car for as long as I did? Without any hesitation,
would I have been able to drive it into the parking

자 한강변을 걸어다니기 시작했고, 그걸 빤히 보고도 나는 계속 바퀴에 뭐가 낀 게 아닐까, 핸들을 이리저리 돌려보며 쭈욱 프라이드에 앉아 있었던 것이다.

결국 혼자 한강변을 돌아다니다가, 매점에 들러 콜라까지 사 마시고 돌아온 여자 후배는, 그때까지도 여전히 운전석에 앉아 기어를 만지작거리고 있던 내 어깨를 통, 치며 말했다.

—에이, 차만 똥차인 줄 알았더니, 선배도 만만치 않네. 다 봤으니까, 이제 가요.

7

이것 또한 물론 다 지나고 난 후에 든 생각이긴 했지만, 만약 삼촌의 프라이드가 그때 아무런 문제도 없었다면, 후진도 전진만큼이나 쭉쭉, 미끄러지듯 잘 되었다면, 다른 차들처럼 띠링 띠링 띠리리리,〈엘리제를 위하여〉선율에 맞춰 부드럽게 잘 되었다면, 그랬다면 내가 그 후로도 오랫동안 그 차를 몰 수 있었을까? 그 차를 몰고 아무렇지도 않게 이마트 주차장에 들어가고, 학교에 가고, 아르바이트로 구한 보습학원에도 가고,

lot of E-mart? To school? To the cram school where I worked part-time? To the *jjimjilbang*? Could I have? Probably not. If it didn't have any problems, then I would've just taken it out a couple of times at night, secretly, and sped down the Jayu Highway or the Naebu Expressway. Because if it didn't have any problems, then I would've been too scared to claim it.

However, after I found out that Uncle's Pride couldn't go in reverse, I thought about it for a few days and the conclusion I reached was that Uncle hadn't left the car—he'd abandoned it. I was certain of it. That was my conclusion. And this time it wasn't just conjecture; it was based on evidence and fact.

One piece of evidence in support of my conclusion came from the opinion of the mechanic I went to see at the Kia Motors service center in Hongje-dong, two days after my night at Han River Park. The mechanic, who had striking silver work sleeves on, took a screwdriver that looked like a long sword and removed the entire bottom part of the center console. Then he lowered himself onto a mechanic's trolley, slid under the body of the Pride, and after inspecting it for a while, told me, "Well,

찜질방에도 가고, 그럴 수 있었을까? 아마, 아마 그러진 못했을 것이다. 만약 그랬다면 나는 기껏해야 야밤에 몰래 빠져나와 자유로나 내부순환로를 몇 번 달려본 후 말았을 것이 분명하다. 아무 문제가 없기 때문에, 오히려 나는 더 조심스러웠을 테니까.

하지만…… 삼촌의 프라이드가 후진이 안 된다는 것을 알게 된 뒤, 나름 며칠을 고민한 후 내린 결론은 '삼촌은 차를 놓고 간 것이 아닌, 버리고 간 것'이었다. 그때 당시 분명, 나는 그렇게 결론을 내렸었다. 그리고 그것은 가정이 아닌, 어떤 근거에 의해서 내린 결론이기도 했는데, 그중 하나에는 한강시민공원을 다녀온 그다음 다음 날이었던가, 프라이드를 몰고 찾아간 기아자동차 홍제동 AS센터의, 은색 토시가 인상적이었던 정비사의 의견도 포함되어 있었다. 정비사는, 대검처럼 기다랗게 생긴 드라이버를 갖고 차량 내부 센터페시아 아래쪽을 모두 뜯어보고 난 후, 그런 다음 다시 밀차에 누워 프라이드 차체 아래로 들어가 한참 동안 무언가를 살펴보고 난 후, 내게 말했다.

—뭐, 문제가 좀 있긴 하지만, 애를 쓰면 고칠 수는 있

there's a problem, but I think with some work I can fix it."

He explained that the rubber gasket in the transmission of Uncle's Pride had worn out so that's why whenever I put the car in reverse, it automatically went into neutral. Once he replaced it, it should go in reverse without a problem. The only problem was the cost of the repairs.

"This is such an early model that if we wanted to replace the rubber gasket, we'd have to replace the entire transmission. Then including the cost of labor..." The mechanic gave the Pride's tire a few tentative kicks. It would cost around 600,000 *won*, he said, and that was only if they could even find the parts they needed. Then very kindly, he told me that the current price for a used Pride was around the 500,000 *won* mark. That was the case for a '90s model Pride, but for an '87 Pride... His voice tapered off. As I took the car keys back from him, I sputtered, "Well, this isn't really my car, it's my uncle's. He didn't want to bother with it so I..."

The second fact to support my belief that Uncle had abandoned his car was the envelope full of papers that I found in the Pride's glove compartment. It contained various documents such as the

겠습니다.

그의 설명에 따르면, 삼촌의 프라이드는 오토미션 쪽에 붙어 있는 패킹이 아예 떨어져나가, 기어를 아무리 'R'로 옮겨도 자동적으로 중립 상태가 된다는 것이었다. 그것만 교체하면 아무 문제없이 후진이 될 거라고 했다. 문제는 비용이었다.

—이게 워낙 초기 모델이어서요, 패킹을 교체하려면 오토미션까지 다 갈아야 하는데 그러면 공임까지 포함해서……

정비사는 툭툭, 타이어를 발로 차면서 60만 원 정도들 거라고 말했다. 그것도 부품을 구할 수 있는 경우에 그렇다는 말이었다. 그러면서 그는 친절하게도 현재 프라이드의 중고 시세가 50만 원 선이라는 것을 가르쳐주었다. 그것도 90년대산 모델의 경우가 그렇지, 87년산 모델은, 하면서 말끝을 흐렸다. 나는 그에게 차 키를 건네받으면서 '사실 이건 내 차가 아니라 우리 삼촌 찬데, 삼촌이 하도 귀찮게 해서……' 운운, 하지 않아도 될 말들을 늘어놓았다.

또 하나의 근거는 프라이드 조수석 콘솔박스에서 나온 서류봉투들이었다. 그 안에는 자동차등록증과 자동

vehicle registration, the road tax receipt, the vehicle insurance, and also two copies of Uncle's resident registration papers and an authentication certificate of Uncle's personal seal. I could understand all the other documents but why the two copies of Uncle's resident registration papers and authentication certificate of his registered personal seal? After thinking about it for a while it finally hit me. They were the documents that were required to have the car scrapped. It was then that I felt like everything had become clear. I didn't know the exact circumstances, but Uncle had found out that the Pride wouldn't go in reverse and so he was asking either Father or me to get rid of it for him. To Uncle, the Pride was like his lover so to get rid of it himself would've been too difficult. And there was the final proof for my conclusion.

What was surprising was that after I came to that conclusion, a sudden sort of courage came over me. You could call it courage, or perhaps even, a kind of relief. Whatever the case, after that day, no, because of that day, I was able to drive Uncle's Pride without any hesitation or any reluctance. Not being able to go in reverse was a drawback, but if anything, that's what made my decision so much

차세 납입영수증, 자동차 보험증서 등과 함께 삼촌의 주민등록초본과 인감증명서가 각각 두 통씩 들어 있었다. 다른 서류들은 다 이해할 수 있었는데, 생뚱맞게 주민등록초본과 인감증명서는 왜 여기 넣어놓으셨을까, 곰곰 고민하다 보니, 아하, 그게 폐차에 필요한 서류라는 것에까지 생각이 닿게 되었다. 그제야 나는 모든 게 명확해진 기분이었다. 어떤 사정 때문인지는 몰라도, 삼촌은 당신의 프라이드가 후진이 되지 않는다는 것을 알게 되었고, 그래서 아버지나 나에게 대신 폐차를 부탁한 것이라는…… 어쨌든 삼촌에겐 애인 같은 프라이드였으니, 당신 손으로 직접 폐차를 하기엔 아무래도 어려운 부분이 있었을 테니까, 뭐 그런 결론……

이상한 것은 그렇게 결론을 내리고 난 뒤부터, 나에게 느닷없이 큰 용기 같은 것이 생겼다는 점이다. 그것을 용기라고 봐도 좋고, 또 어떤 안도감 같은 것이라고 해도 틀린 말은 아닐 것이다. 어쨌든 나는 그다음부터, 아니 그 덕분에, 삼촌의 프라이드를 주저 없이, 거리낌 없이 몰고 다닐 수 있게 되었으니까. 후진이 안 된다는 단점이 있었지만, 오히려 그것이 나에겐 더 편안하게 다

easier. The reality was that while driving around in Seoul, there really was no need to go in reverse unless you were parking. Plus, I was still a new driver so parking was already difficult for me (when I banged up the Sonata's side mirror and rear bumper, both times were when I was trying to reverse park). But with Uncle's Pride, since all I needed to do was get out and push, there was no need for me to stress out over parking. When I was parking at the E-mart, at school, at the cram school, or at the *jjimjilbang*, all I needed to do was push the car into the parking stall and push it back out again (after about a month, I mastered how to get out of the driver's seat and control the steering wheel while going in reverse so parallel parking was no longer a problem).

As I pushed the Pride back and forth by its trunk day after day, I found myself gradually getting used to the car. Even when I was reading a book in the middle of the night, I'd go out for a drive down the Jayu Highway, and on my way home after finishing work at the cram school, I'd turn the wheel and head towards the Seoul Ring Expressway. On some days, I'd get a little greedy and go all the way to Cheonan. And, on other days, I'd drive at an average speed of 130km/hr and drive all the way to

가온 것도 사실이었다. 사실, 서울 시내에선 주차를 할 경우를 빼곤 후진을 할 일은 거의 없었다. 더구나 그때까지도 나는 주차가 제일 어려운 초보 운전자였다(소나타의 사이드미러와 뒷범퍼를 깨먹은 것도 모두 후진 주차를 하다가 생긴 일들이었다). 하지만, 삼촌의 프라이드는 주차를 할 일이 생기면 무조건 나와서 밀기만 하면 되었으니까, 따로 신경을 곤두세울 일 같은 것은 없었다. 그저, 이마트에서도 밀고, 학교에서도 밀고, 학원에서도 밀고, 찜질방에서도 밀고. 무조건 밀어서 차를 넣고, 무조건 밀어서 차를 빼면 되는 것이었다(한 달 정도 지난 후부턴 운전석 문을 열고 핸들을 조작하면서 미는 방법도 터득하게 되었다. 그러니, 일렬 주차도 아무 문제 없었던 것이다). 그렇게 매일매일 트렁크 부분을 밀다 보니, 어느새 나는 조금씩 조금씩 프라이드에 적응해나가게 되었다. 나는 한밤중, 책을 읽다가도 말고 집 밖으로 나와 자유로를 달렸으며, 학원 강의를 끝내고 집으로 돌아가다 말고 핸들을 돌려 외곽순환도로를 달리기도 했다. 어떤 날은 조금 더 욕심을 내서 천안까지 갔다 오기도 했고, 또 어떤 날은 시속 130킬로미터로 꾸준히 달려 안면도까지 내려간 다음, 혼자 바지락칼국수를 먹고 돌아오기도 했

Anmyeon Island, eat a bowl of noodles with manila clams, then come back home. After about two months of driving Uncle's Pride, I started to take night drives along the expressways probably three times a week.

I rarely turned on the stereo when I drove. At first, it was because I didn't trust the battery. But after that, it was because I didn't want to get distracted by music or by any other sounds. I only wanted to listen to the sounds the car made. If you ask me why I drove around so much, even now, I can't think of a solid reason. But if I really had to give an answer, then I think I'd say I wanted to sort of see where the limits were. Every day when I started the engine of the Pride, I'd tell myself over and over that today would be the last day. Or maybe it was a sort of psychological reactance—since it was a car that couldn't go in reverse, then let's take it forward even farther, even faster. Roads were built to be driven forward on and there was no reversing on expressways. I began to wonder if Uncle had thought the same way. That perhaps that was why he had stayed in the Pride for so long. That perhaps he had traveled forward so far that he'd forgotten where to go back to. A state of mild

다. 삼촌의 프라이드를 몰기 시작한 지 두 달 정도 지난 뒤부터는 나는 거의 일주일에 세 번꼴로 밤의 고속도로를 달렸다. 달리면서 나는 오디오도 거의 켜지 않았다. 처음엔 배터리가 미덥지 못해서 그랬지만, 그 뒤로는 그저 다른 어떤 소음들에도 방해받지 않고, 오직 차가 내는 소리를 듣기 위해서, 음악을 틀지 않게 되었다. 왜 그렇게 달렸냐고 묻는다면 지금도 딱히 대답할 말은 생각나지 않는다. 그러나 그래도 굳이 답을 해야 한다면 무언가 한계 같은 것을 보고 싶어서 그랬던 것 같기도 하다. 그때 당시엔 매일매일 프라이드에 시동을 걸면서 오늘이 마지막일 거야, 오늘이 마지막일 거야, 라고 중얼거렸으니까. 그도 아니면 어떤 반발심리 같은 게 있었을지도 모른다. 뒤로는 못 가는 자동차이니, 어쨌든 앞으로는 최대한 멀리, 최대한 빨리 가보자는…… 고속도로는 후진할 수 없는 길이니까, 무조건 앞으로만 나가야 하는 길이니까…… 그러면서 나는 얼핏얼핏 삼촌도 나와 비슷한 게 아니었을까, 그래서 그토록 오랜 세월 프라이드에서만 머문 게 아니었을까, 하는 생각을 하기도 했다. 달리다 보니까 돌아갈 곳을 아예 잊어버린 게 아닐까, 하는…… 일종의 당혹감 같은 것 말이다.

bewilderment you might say.

Of course these thoughts only appeared in brief flashes, and only lasted until I discovered Uncle's notebooks.

8

I found them, four notebooks bound tightly with wire, in the trunk of the Pride under the spare tire. I was heading home after school one day when the driver in the next lane kept pointing at me. I got out and saw that the left back tire was lying flat on the ground like a deflated balloon. Driving at minimal speed in the "slow" lane, I took the car back to the Kia Motors service center in Hongje-dong. When they opened the trunk to take out the spare tire, there were Uncle's notebooks. At this point it had been about half a year since I'd started driving Uncle's Pride.

It was a sort of "car-keeping ledger." Inside Uncle's notebooks, starting with the first entry on October 16, 1987, each line contained a record of the departure point, a middle rest stop, the final destination, the total travel distance, the total gas consumption, etc. For example, this is what one entry

물론 그런 생각들은 내가 삼촌의 노트를 발견하기 전까지, 그것도 아주 잠깐잠깐씩만, 하게 된 것에 불과했지만.

8

삼촌의, 철심으로 단단하게 묶은 네 권짜리 대학노트가 나온 곳은 프라이드 트렁크의 예비 타이어 바로 아랫부분에서였다. 학교에서 집으로 돌아오는 길에 옆 차선 운전사가 계속 손짓을 해서 내려보니, 이런, 왼쪽 뒷바퀴가 바람 빠진 풍선처럼 주저앉아 있었다. 최대한 저속으로 일차선으로만 달려 다시 기아자동차 홍제동 AS센터에 도착해 트렁크에 들어 있던 예비 타이어를 빼내보니, 그 아래 삼촌의 노트가 들어 있었다. 내가 삼촌의 프라이드를 몰기 시작한 지 거의 반년 정도 흐른 뒤의 일이었다.

그것은 일종의 '차계부'와도 같은 것이었다. 87년 10월 16일부터 씌어지기 시작한 삼촌의 노트엔 한 줄 한 줄, 그날의 출발지와 중간 도착지, 최종 도착지, 총 운행거

looked like:

1987/10/27 Guro-dong depart→Ahyeon-dong→Bucheon Chunui-dong→Guro-dong arrival (total 63km, Chunui gas station 10L, 5,420 *won*)

Uncle had written nothing else in the notebooks. Occasionally, some pages had records of tire changes, oil changes, a service center phone number, etc. But other than that, Uncle had kept only a comprehensive record of the distance the Pride had traveled and the locations the Pride had stopped at. For a long time, I read Uncle's notebooks, read them again and again, but there wasn't really much that I could decipher. I skimmed through the pages in the hopes of finding any scribbled notes, but there was nothing. The notebooks only contained figures and destination names, written neatly in straight blocks.

According to Uncle's notes, for the first month he'd driven the Pride, he'd traveled back and forth between Guro-dong, Seoul and Chunui-dong, Bucheon. This continued up until the Christmas of that year but changed shortly after. Guro-dong and Chunui-dong disappeared and were replaced by

리와 주유량 등이 적혀 있었다. 일테면 이런 식이었다.

1987 10/27 구로동 출발 → 아현동 → 부천 춘의동 →
구로동 도착(총 63㎞, 춘의주유소 10 ℓ 5,420원)

거기엔 그 외 다른 어떤 문장들도 포함되어 있지 않
았다. 간간이 타이어 교체와 엔진오일 교체, 공업사 전
화번호 등이 적혀 있는 페이지가 나오긴 했지만, 그것
을 제외하곤 삼촌은 철저하게 프라이드가 달린 거리만,
프라이드가 머문 장소만 기록해두었다. 나는 오랫동안
삼촌의 그 노트들을 읽고, 또 읽어보았지만, 그것만으
로는 해석할 수 있는 것이 그리 많지 않았다. 어디 한 귀
퉁이에 낙서라도 돼 있지 않을까, 찾아보았지만, 그런
것은 아무것도 없었다. 오직 반듯반듯한 정자로 씌어진
숫자와 지명만으로 이루어진 노트였다.

노트에 따르면 삼촌은 프라이드를 몰기 시작한 처음
한 달 동안은 거의 매일 구로동과 부천 춘의동 사이만
을 왔다 갔다 반복했다. 그러던 것이 그해 크리스마스
를 전후로 해서 바뀌기 시작했는데, 구로동과 부천 춘

various places such as Muju and Daechon, Samcheok and Hwajinpo, and Tongyeong and Yeosu, but there was no consistent pattern. During that period, there was a time when the Pride traveled an incredible 700km in one day and another when it gassed up two times in the same day at 30L each time. In some places the dates were missing in sections, so he probably hadn't driven the Pride on those days. But even then, those periods of relative inactivity lasted for only about four days with the longest period not going over ten days. After that, the Pride resumed its wanderings from Gochang to Gimcheon, Ulsan to Jecheon, and Namwon to Yeonggwang. However, even on the day that it traveled to Gapyeong, the final destination was recorded as Hwachcon, Gangwon-do.

The notebooks reestablished a consistent pattern beginning in February of '88 and continued for the next two years; the Pride only wandered around Cheongju. But that didn't imply that Uncle lived in Cheongju since it was only listed as a rest stop, not a final destination. The final destinations were recorded as Chungju, Wonju, and Janghowon. This pattern of longer sojourns was also recorded between 1994 and 1996 in the Namyangju vicinity,

의동은 사라지고, 대신 무주와 대천, 삼척과 화진포, 통영과 여수 등 여러 갈래로, 일정한 패턴 없이 나누어졌다. 그때 당시 프라이드는 어떤 날은 하루 동안 무려 7백 킬로미터를 달리기도 했고, 총 30리터씩 두 번 주유한 날도 있었다. 또 어떤 때는 날짜가 뭉텅뭉텅 비어 있는 칸도 있었는데, 그땐 아마도 운행을 하지 않은 것 같았다. 하지만 그것도 길어야 나흘, 가장 길었던 기간은 열흘을 넘기지 않았다. 그 뒤로는 다시 고창과 김천, 울산과 제천, 남원과 영광 등으로 프라이드는 떠돌기 시작했다. 가평에 온 것으로 기록된 날에도, 그러나 프라이드의 최종 도착지는 강원도 화천으로 적혀 있었다.

노트에 다시 일정한 패턴이 나타나기 시작한 것은 88년 2월부터였는데, 그때부터 프라이드는 줄곧 2년간 청주 근처에서만 떠돌았다. 하지만 그렇다고 삼촌이 청주에 살았던 것은 아닌 것 같았는데, 청주는 매번 중간 도착지였지, 최종 도착지는 아니었기 때문이었다. 그때에도 최종 도착지는 충주와 원주, 장호원 등지로 따로 적혀 있었다. 그런 패턴은 다시 94년에서부터 96년까지 남양주 부근에서 한 번, 99년 하반기에 광명시 철산동을 기점으로 한 번 이루어지다가, 2001년부터는 줄곧

again in the second half of 1999, centering around Cheolsan-dong, Gwangmyeong city, and from 2001, it remained constant with Hadong, Gyeong-sangnam-do as its center. One time, remembering Uncle's notebooks, I'd asked Father if we had any distant relatives living in Hadong. My father replied, "Since the beginning, no one in our household has ever gone farther than Anseong. What I mean is, our household has never *dropped* below that.

For some reason, I'd felt really embarrassed by the way Father had said it, but it didn't seem like Father did.

The last entry recorded in Uncle's notebooks was this:

2004/4/5 Hadong→Hadong (total 5km)

2004/4/6 Hadong→Hongeun-dong, Seoul (total 412km, Jeongan Rest Area gas station 32L, 45,000 *won*. Seo-daemun gas station 36L, 50,000 *won*)

After I saw that entry, I began to vaguely wonder if maybe Uncle hadn't abandoned the Pride in front of our house. That maybe, he was returning it. At that time, Grandmother was definitely living with us

경남 하동을 중심으로 이어졌다. 언젠가 한번, 삼촌의 노트가 생각나 아버지에게 혹 먼 친척 중 하동에 사는 사람이 있냐고, 물어본 적이 있었다. 그러자 아버지는 이렇게 말했다.

─우리 집안은 옛부터 안성 아래로는 단 한 번도 내려간 적이 없었다. 대대로 귀양을 안 갔다는 얘기지.

나는 어쩐지 그 말이 좀 부끄럽게 여겨졌지만, 아버지는 그렇게 생각하지 않는 것 같았다.

삼촌의 노트의 맨 마지막 페이지에 나와 있는 기록은 다음과 같았다.

2004 4/5 하동 → 하동(총 5㎞)

2004 4/6 하동 → 서울 홍은동(총 412㎞, 정안휴게소 주유소 32 *l* 45,000원, 서대문주유소 36 *l* 50,000원)

나는 그 기록을 본 뒤부터 막연히 삼촌이 우리 집에 프라이드를 버리고 간 것이 아닌, 돌려주고 간 것이 아닐까, 생각하게 되었다. 그때 할머니가 있는 곳은 분명 우리 집이었으니까, 어쩌면, 어쩌면…… 하지만 그런

so maybe, just maybe... But that thought some-times brought with it slightly more frightening thoughts and it wasn't just me, but Grandmother who thought them too.

Whenever Grandmother saw the Pride she'd ask me, "Hey, hey. The car isn't dead, right?" And whenever Grandmother asked me this I'd tell her that the real problem was that it was still running too well.

"Hey, hey. Make sure you take good care of it, okay? Make sure you keep it well fed until your uncle gets back."

As she said this, she'd hand me a crumpled 10,000 *won* bill. I took the money from her and asked, "What about me? You'll give the car allow-ance but not your own grandson?"

Grandmother never replied.

9

The fact that Uncle might have had a girlfriend in Hadong became known to me a year later. Auntie had mentioned it one morning in the Pride. I was slowly maneuvering the car, looking for a place to eat breakfast with Auntie, who had stayed up the

생각은 또 어쩔 수 없이 때때로 조금 불길한 마음으로
도 이어지곤 했는데, 그런 마음은 비단 나뿐만이 아닌
할머니도 마찬가지였던 것 같다. 할머니는 삼촌의 프라
이드를 볼 때마다 내게 물었다.

　　—야 야, 저게 안 굴러가는 건 아니지?

　　그때마다 나는 할머니에게 너무 잘 굴러가서 문제라
고 말해주었다.

　　—야 야, 네가 관리를 잘해라, 응? 네 삼촌 올 때까지
기름도 잘 먹여주고.

　　할머니는 그러면서 내게 꼬깃꼬깃 구겨진 만 원짜리
지폐 한 장을 내밀었다. 나는 가만히 할머니에게서 그
돈을 받아들었다. 그리고 말했다.

　　—나는? 자동차한텐 용돈 주고, 손주한텐 안 줘?

　　할머니는 말이 없었다.

9

　　하동에 삼촌의 애인이 살고 있을지도 모른다고 한 것
은 그로부터 다시 1년이 지난 후, 우연히 함께 프라이드
를 탄 고모의 입에서 흘러나온 말이었다. 그때 나는, 전

entire night taking care of Grandmother in her hospital room. It looked like she hadn't been able to sleep at all and her eyes were bloodshot. When she got into the passenger seat of the Pride she burst into loud sobs that left me feeling powerless.

Grandmother had lung cancer. The tumor had spread through almost half of one lung, and nobody knew when it would spread to the other lung. There was no telling how the family was really taking it, but it seemed like they had come to terms with it, at least outwardly, since Grandmother had just passed eighty. And it was the same for Grandmother. It was probably the third day of her hospitalization. It was my turn to sleep on the folding bed in her hospital room. At around midnight, Grandmother poked me in the shoulder.

"Hey, hey. Are you sleeping? How is it that you're older now but you still fall asleep so early in the evening?"

I lay on my side and faced Grandmother and asked her, if midnight was early evening, then what time exactly did she consider nighttime? Then I started teasing her about how, even at her age, she could talk so much and that one day, even her dentures would fall out in mid-sentence.

날 할머니가 입원한 병실에서 밤을 새운 고모를 데리고 어디 아침식사를 할 만한 식당이 없나, 핸들을 잡은 채 두리번거리고 있던 중이었다. 고모는 밤새 한숨도 못 잔 듯, 두 눈이 벌겋게 충혈되어 있었는데, 프라이드 조수석에 올라타자마자 엉엉 큰 소리로 울음을 터뜨려 나를 한동안 이도 저도 못 하게 만들었다.

할머니는 폐암이었다. 이미 한쪽 폐는 암덩어리들이 반 이상 퍼져나간 상태였고, 나머지 한쪽도 언제 어느 때 이상이 생길지 알 수 없는 상태였다. 할머니는 그때 이미 여든을 넘긴 무렵인지라 가족들은 그 속마음까지야 어떤지 알 순 없었으나, 적어도 겉모습만큼은 모두들 무덤덤하게 받아들이는 눈치였다. 그리고 그건 할머니도 마찬가지인 것 같았다. 입원 사흘째 되던 날인가, 그날은 내가 보조침대에 누워 병실에서 잠을 잤는데, 자정 무렵쯤 할머니가 톡톡, 내 어깨를 두들겼다.

—야 야, 자냐? 넌 어떻게 된 애가 나이가 들어도 그렇게 초저녁잠이 많냐?

나는 할머니 쪽으로 모로 누우면서, 자정이 초저녁이면 도대체 진짜 저녁은 몇 시냐며, 할머니는 어떻게 된 게 연세를 그렇게 잡수셔도 말이 그리 많냐고, 그러다

Then Grandmother craned her neck closer to me and said, "Hey, hey. It's cancer, right? They said it's cancer?"

I stared at Grandmother's IV for a moment and then answered, "Yeah, it's cancer. But they said it's smaller than a pea so they can't even really see it."

"Hey, hey. It's sad, isn't it? Isn't it really sad?"

"What is? You having cancer? Well it's still smaller than a pea. They said that all you need to do is take medication."

I said this in a small voice.

"No, no. Not me. The cancer. Of all the people, it came into this old body. Hey, hey. They say that when cancer comes into an old body, it doesn't have enough energy to even grow properly. Do you remember Deok-hyeong's grandmother? The one who lived in Deokjeok Valley? She got cancer at eighty-four and lived until ninety-five. Poor cancer."

In the middle of her story, Grandmother even paused to laugh, but I choked up for a second because I felt like she was doing it on purpose, for my sake. So when Auntie started to bawl like a little child the moment she stepped into the Pride I thought, she must be feeling exactly the way I did.

가 틀니도 다 달아나버린다고, 버릇없이 놀렸다.

—야 야, 암 맞다지? 암이라지?

할머니는 내 쪽으로 고개를 조금 더 내밀면서 물었다.

—응, 암 맞대. 한데, 아직 콩알만 해서 잘 보이지도 않는대.

나는 할머니의 링거를 쳐다보면서 그렇게 말했다.

—야 야, 불쌍해서 어쩌냐? 불쌍해서 어째?

—누가? 할머니가? 아직 콩알만 하다는데 뭐…… 약 먹으면 된대.

나는 조금 작은 목소리로 말했다.

—아니, 아니, 나 말고, 암 말이야, 암. 하필 다 늙은 몸에 들어와서…… 야 야, 늙은 몸에 들어온 암은 기력이 없어서 잘 자라지도 못한단다. 왜 거 덕적골 덕형이 할머니도 여든넷인가에 암에 걸렸는데 아흔다섯에 갔잖아. 암만 죽어난 거지.

할머니는 이야기를 하는 도중 낄낄, 웃기까지 했는데, 나는 그게 나를 위해 일부러 그러는 것만 같아 잠깐 울컥하기도 했다. 그러니까 고모가 프라이드에 올라타자마자 어린아이처럼 큰 소리로 울기 시작한 것 역시 나와 크게 다르진 않을 거라고, 나는 생각했다. 더구나 반

To make matters worse, it was also around that time that Auntie had gotten a divorce from her police officer husband and had started living alone in an apartment, separated from her kids. Auntie kept crying, saying that it was all her fault Grandmother had gotten sick, that it was because she'd caused Grandmother so much grief.

I felt like I needed to change the subject so after she calmed down a bit, I asked her about Uncle.

"Hey, Auntie? Do you know anyone who lives in Hadong?"

Auntie sniffled and replied through her tears, "In Hadong? There's nobody in Hadong. Why do you ask?"

"Well up until recently, it seemed like Uncle was in and around that area."

As if she'd never been crying, Auntie turned to me wide-eyed and asked, "Your Uncle? Why? Did somebody see him?"

"No, there was a record of it in a notebook that I found in his car. I wondered if maybe Uncle had a friend living there."

"There's nobody in Hadong. But, whatever the case is, I wonder if your uncle even knows that your grandmother is lying like this in the hospital.

년 전 경찰관인 고모부와 이혼한 고모는, 그즈음 아이들과도 떨어져 작은 아파트에 혼자 살고 있던 처지였다. 고모는 계속 울면서 자기 때문에 할머니가 병이 난 거라고, 자기가 속을 썩여 그런 것이라고 자책했다.

나는 화제를 좀 다른 곳으로 돌려야 할 것 같아서, 고모의 울음이 조금 진정되고 난 후, 삼촌의 얘기를 물었다.

─근데 고모, 혹시 하동에 누가 사나?

고모는 콧물을 훌쩍거리며 하동에 있긴 누가 있다고 그래, 라고 울음 섞인 목소리로 대답했다.

─한데, 그건 왜?

─아니, 삼촌이 얼마 전까지 그곳을 계속 다닌 것 같아서.

─오빠가? 왜? 누가 봤대?

고모는 언제 울었냐는 듯, 두 눈을 크게 뜨고 내게 물었다.

─아니, 그냥 차에 그런 기록이 남아 있어서…… 거기 삼촌 친구나 누구 아는 사람이 있는가 해서.

─하동에 누가 있다고…… 에휴. 그러나저러나 네 삼촌은 네 할머니 저러고 누워 있는지 알기나 하는지, 하여간 진짜……

Honestly..."

Auntie gave her nose a huge blow, then fell silent.

I spotted a 24 hour *chueotang* spot and was just about to turn the wheel when Auntie nearly hollered in my ear, "Oh my God! The girl! *She* must have been living there. Hey! I heard that her hometown was somewhere in Gyeongsang-do. It's got to be her!"

10

That day, what Auntie told me was the same story of Uncle that Grandmother had told me over and over again, but her version was a bit different. According to Auntie, it was true that when he worked at the factory, it was as if he didn't exist. But every day after work, he went to some kind of gathering and returned home at dawn. Later on, she learned that the official name of the gathering was the "Guro-dong Worker's Labor Union," and sometimes, the group gathered at the one-room rental that Uncle and Auntie shared. Mainly, they met and read poetry or novels, even newspaper articles together, then held a discussion. A couple of times, Auntie

고모는 큰 소리로 코를 한 번 푼 후, 한동안 말이 없었다.

그리고 내가 24시간 추어탕집을 하나 발견하고 그쪽으로 막 핸들을 돌렸을 때, 고모는 소리치듯 큰 소리로 말했다.

—어머, 어머, 그 여자! 그 여자가 거기 있는가 보다, 애! 그 여자 고향이 경상도 어디라고 했는데, 그 여자가 맞나봐!

10

그날, 고모에게서 들은 얘기는, 내가 예전 할머니에게서 듣고 듣고 또 들었던 삼촌의 얘기와는 조금 차이가 있는 것이었다. 고모에 따르면, 그때 당시 삼촌은 공장에선 있는 듯 없는 듯 지낸 건 맞지만, 일이 끝나고 나면 매일 어느 모임에 나가 새벽 무렵에나 돌아왔다고 했다. 나중에 알게 된 그 모임의 정확한 명칭은 '구로동일꾼노동자회'였는데, 가끔 삼촌과 고모가 살고 있던 자취방으로도 사람들이 모였다고 했다. 주로 함께 모여 시도 읽고 소설도 읽고 신문기사도 읽으며 토론을 하는

had gone home and ended up sitting in on the get-togethers. For the first time in her life, she heard names such as Kim Ji-ha, Cho Se-hui, and Jeon Tae-il. But instead of these people, it was a girl, a single girl, who had caught her attention. The girl had her hair in a bob and wore round, horn-rimmed glasses. She was a tall, slender girl with dark skin, and she worked at a textiles factory. Even among all the men, she stood her ground and spoke in a low, heavy voice, and when they sometimes drank *makgeolli* together, she'd be the first one to drum the table with her chopsticks and sing "Jinju-nanggun." After Auntie attended a few of the gatherings, she intuitively knew that Uncle liked the girl. She also found out that after every meeting, Uncle escorted the girl all the way to her place in Bucheon, and then came back home. Auntie had no problem with that. She thought if things went well, she would be getting a sister-in-law soon. But what was a problem was the time. After working overtime, the group gathered at around 10pm and finished at around midnight. On the way there, it was possible to catch the last train. But on the way back, it was usually so late that you were guaranteed to have to walk back.

모임이었다. 자취방에 들어갔다가 몇 번 얼떨결에 모임에 참석하게 된 고모는 그곳에서 김지하니, 조세희니, 전태일이니, 난생처음 듣는 이름들을 알게 되었는데, 사실 그 사람들보다는 한 여자, 한 여자에게만 자꾸 눈길이 갔다고 했다. 단발머리에 동그란 뿔테 안경을 쓴, 키가 껑충하게 크고 피부도 거무튀튀한, 방직공장에 다니는 처녀였다. 남자들 틈에서도 기죽지 않고 괄괄한 목소리로 말을 하고, 가끔 함께 막걸리를 마실 때는 누구보다 먼저 젓가락으로 밥상을 두들기며 〈진주낭군〉을 부르던 여자였는데, 고모는 모임에 몇 번 참석하고 난 뒤, 삼촌이 그녀를 좋아하고 있다는 것을 직감적으로 알아챘다고 했다. 매번 모임이 끝난 후, 삼촌이 다시 부천에 있는 그녀의 자취방까지 바래다주고 온다는 사실 또한 알게 되었고…… 거기까지야 고모도 뭐 그러려니, 잘만 하면 금세 올케언니가 생기겠구나 생각했는데, 한데, 한데, 문제는 시간이었다. 잔업을 끝내고 사람들이 모이는 시간은 대략 밤 10시 전후, 그리고 모임이 끝나는 시간은 자정 무렵이었다. 어찌어찌 갈 때는 막차를 타고 간다고 해도, 돌아올 땐 영락없이 걸어서 와야 하는 시간이었다.

"Back then, your uncle was always falling asleep. Even when working at the factory, he kept nodding off so he was always dropping the fabric that rolled out of the pressing machine. Whenever he got a Sunday off, he didn't even eat and just slept all day. Of course they noticed at the factory. The manager called your uncle out separately and warned him that if he kept it up, he'd be sent to the mixing room. People said that being sent to the mixing room was pretty much a death sentence because they used toxic chemicals like formamide or something. And once you're exposed to it, you suffer dizzy spells and stuff."

But what made Auntie madder was the girl's attitude. For sure, it didn't seem like the girl didn't like Uncle, but it also didn't seem like she regarded him particularly more. On their days off, she didn't see them going on dates and there was no gift giving or exchanging of letters between them. Then Auntie's voice got louder as she explained how the girl should've just been straightforward with him. Uncle was sacrificing his sleep to escort her all the way home and she wouldn't even give him a straightaway yes or no. What was she doing? Was she testing him out?

—네 삼촌은 그때 늘 조는 게 일이었어. 공장에서도 계속 꾸벅꾸벅 조는 바람에 프레스기에서 나오는 원단을 툭툭, 놓치기 일쑤였고…… 그래서 어쩌다 아무 일도 없는 일요일이 돌아오면 하루 종일 아무것도 먹지 않고 잠만 잔 거야. 그러니, 공장에서도 좋아할 일이 없지 뭐야. 주임은 삼촌을 따로 불러 자꾸 그러면 배합실로 보내버린다고 하고…… 그땐 배합실로 가면 다들 죽는다고 했거든. 거긴 무슨 포름아미드인가 뭔가, 하도 독한 약을 써대는 바람에 들어가는 족족 어지럼병을 얻고 그랬거든.

고모가 더 화가 났던 건, 여자의 태도 때문이었다. 여자는 분명 삼촌을 싫어하는 것 같지는 않았는데, 그렇다고 더 특별하게 여기는 눈치도 아닌 것 같았다. 일 없는 날 둘이 따로 만나는 것 같지도 않았고, 선물을 주고받거나 편지를 건네는 일도 없었다고 했다. 그럼, 차라리 딱 부러지게 말을 하든지, 사람이 밤잠 못 자면서 그렇게 먼 길을 바래다주는데, 이거다 저거다 말도 안 하고, 사람을 재보는 것도 아니고 말이야…… 고모는 그 대목에서 목소리를 높이기도 했다.

—그래서 내가 생각해보니까, 우리 오빠가 중졸이잖

"So I thought about it, and, you know your uncle's a high school dropout, right? I kept on thinking that maybe that's what the girl was worried about. From what I could gather, the girl was pretty smart and she was a good talker. In contrast, your uncle never said a word and always just sat there dozing off. Then when the meeting finished, he'd suddenly get up, zip up his jacket, and follow the girl out. So even in my eyes, it was a bit pathetic."

That's when Auntie came up with the idea to buy Uncle a car. If he had a car, then it wouldn't take too long even if he dropped the girl off and came back home, and if that were the case, then the manager would get off his back at the factory and he wouldn't be sent to the mixing room. And even from the girl's perspective, she'd think, sure, he isn't very educated, but he must have at least a few acres of land to inherit in the countryside. This was how Auntie had summed up the situation. So, from that moment on, Auntie told, sort of embellished the story of Uncle and his mystery girl and started to steadily egg Grandmother on. It was also around this time when she told Grandmother that Uncle was so invisible to people that they responded with, "Oh really? There's someone like that?" when

니? 그 여자가 그게 마음에 걸려서 그러나, 자꾸 그런 생각이 들더라구. 그때 그 여자는, 내가 간간이 보니까 아는 것도 많고, 말도 무척 잘하더라구. 반면에 우리 오빠는 매번 아무 말도 없이 앉아 있다가 꾸벅꾸벅 졸기나 하고…… 그러다가 끝나면 화들짝 일어나 점퍼를 꿰입고 졸졸 여자 뒤나 따라가고…… 그러니, 내가 봐도 좀 답답해 보이더라구.

그래서 그때 고모가 생각해낸 게 바로 자동차였다. 작은 자동차라도 한 대 있다면 배웅을 해주고 와도 시간이 얼마 안 걸릴 것이고, 그렇게 되면 공장에서 조는 일도 없을 테니까 배합실로 쫓겨나는 일도 없을 것 같았다. 또 여자의 입장에서도, 아, 이 사람이 배운 건 없어도, 그래도 고향집에 물려받을 논마지기는 좀 있구나, 생각하지 않을까, 하는…… 그게 고모의 계산이었다. 그래서 고모는 그때부터 조금 과장해서, 부풀려서, 계속 할머니를 부추기기 시작한 것이었다. 할머니에게 삼촌이 '어머, 그런 사람이 있었어?'라고 말해진다고 한 것도 그즈음의 일이었고.

하지만, 정작 삼촌이 프라이드를 갖게 된 이후부터,

he was mentioned.

But after Uncle got his Pride, Auntie's memories, starting from that point, were the same as being practically non-existent. Auntie explained that it was probably the day right after Uncle drove the car up from Gapyeong. She vaguely remembered seeing him just once giving the girl a ride back after their meeting had finished, but for whatever reason, she strangely couldn't remember anything after that.

I found out the reason later on, and there was nothing strange about it—Auntie had also fallen in love. She'd fallen hard for a guy and didn't make it home most nights so, of course, for the next two months, the two months starting from when Uncle got his Pride until he quit his job at the factory, there was no way that Auntie could've known what was happening with Uncle. In no way was Auntie at fault for this. Auntie was twenty-three years old at the time. Twenty-three. The age where if she didn't absolutely need to go home, then it was only natural that she wouldn't. Twenty-three. The age where if you fell in love, you would want to spend every moment talking about anything and everything. Twenty-three. The age when only the present day

그다음부터 고모의 기억은 거의, 아무것도 없는 편이나 마찬가지였다. 가평에서 직접 프라이드를 몰고 온 다음 날이던가, 딱 한 번 모임이 끝난 후, 여자를 태우던 삼촌의 모습을 지켜본 것도 같은데, 어쩌된 일인지 그다음부턴 이상하게 아무것도 기억나지 않는다는 것이 고모의 설명이었다. 후에 내가 알게 된 것이지만, 사실 그건 전혀 이상한 일이 아니었다. 그땐 고모 역시 사랑에 빠져 있는 상태였으니까, 한 남자에게 빠져 거의 매일 자취방으로 돌아오지 못하고 있던 처지였으니까, 그러니…… 그 두 달 동안, 그러니까 프라이드를 갖게 된 시점부터 공장을 그만두게 된 순간까지, 삼촌에게 무슨 일이 벌어졌는지 알 수가 없었던 것이다. 그건 또한, 당연히 고모의 잘못도 아니었다. 고모는 그때 스물세 살이었다. 자취방으로 돌아가지 않아도 된다면, 돌아가지 않는 게 당연한 스물세 살, 사랑하는 사람이 생기면 모든 걸 쉴 새 없이 이야기하고픈 스물세 살, 하루하루만 의미 있는 스물세 살, 그 스물세 살 말이다.

holds any significance. That's the type of age twenty-three was.

11

Samjeon Automobile Service Center was a car repair shop on the first floor of a warehouse building. It had a sidewalk sign right in front of the building with the words "FLAT TIRE" and "CAR WRECK SPECIALIST" painted on it with big red letters. In order to get there, you had to take the subway to Yeongdeungpo Station and walk 500 meters, keeping the Lotte Department Store at your back. It was one of those businesses that you'd expect to still see running, as long as nothing in particular happened to it. It was also Uncle's regular repair shop.

I decided I should pay a visit because of a problem with the Pride's brake pedal. It had probably been about two years since I'd started driving the Pride. For some reason, whenever I pressed the brake pedal and released it, the pedal wouldn't return to its original position unless I forced it back into position by pulling it with my foot. But this was something serious, not just something like not be-

지금도 별다른 일이 없으면 영업을 하고 있을 게 분명한 '삼전자동차공업사'는, 영등포역에서 내려 롯데백화점을 등지고 왼쪽으로 5백 미터쯤 가면 나오는, 창고형 건물 1층에 자리잡은 자동차정비소이다. 건물 바로 앞에 '빵꾸' '렉카 전문'이라고 붉은색 페인트로 크게 쓴 입간판을 내놓고 있는 그 공업사는, 사실 삼촌의 단골 정비소이기도 했다.

내가 그곳을 한번 찾아가봐야겠다고 마음먹은 것은 프라이드의 브레이크 페달에 생긴 문제 때문이었다. 프라이드를 몬 지 2년째 되어가던 시점이던가, 어찌된 일인지 브레이크를 밟았다가 떼도, 페달이 원위치로 되돌아오지 않는 문제가 생긴 적이 있었다. 발등으로 다시 페달을 밀어올리면 그제야 제자리로 되돌아오곤 했지만, 그건 후진이 안 되는 것과는 차원이 다른, 심각한 문제였다. 자칫하다간 앞으로도 갈 수 없는 일이 생길 수 있으니까…… 그래서 그때 나는 잠깐, 어쩌면 이젠 정말 한계가 온 것일지도 모른다고 그만 포기할까 생각하기도 했었는데, 한데, 한데, 그게 쉽지가 않았다. 프라이

ing able to go in reverse. If I wasn't careful, I could end up not being able to go forward either.

So, momentarily, I thought that perhaps this was really the end and that I should just give up. But, but, it wasn't that simple. Grandmother regarded the Pride like it was Uncle, and for me personally, over the years, I had unknowingly grown very attached to it as well. Sure, my students at the cram school called me "the pushcart driver" and the DD service drivers always bitched about having to drive "this piece of crap." (I admit it was my fault. When a driver said it wouldn't go in reverse I'd said to him, "Mister, all you need to do is push it. Push as hard as you can." So it was understandable that he swore at me.) But to me, the Pride had become something like my first love. More frequently, and for no apparent reason, I started to feel sad and melancholic whenever I looked at the Pride.

One time in winter after a heavy snowfall, I watched the Pride, parked in the side of an alley, become slowly buried under a heap of snow. Without being aware of it, I actually shed a few tears. (Unfortunately, my father saw me. He probably thought I was crying at the bitter thought of having to push the car around in the snow. The next day, Father told Moth-

드를 삼촌처럼 여기는 할머니도 할머니였지만, 나 역시
도 그간 알게 모르게 정이 많이 들었기 때문이었다. 학
원 제자들에겐 '리어카라이더'라는 소리를 듣기도 하고,
대리운전 기사에겐 '별 거지 같은 차(물론 내가 먼저 잘못
을 하긴 했다. 후진이 안 된다는 기사에게 "아저씨, 힘껏 미시면
됩니다! 힘껏 미세요"라고 말했으니, 욕먹어도 할 말은 없는 것이
다)'라는 말을 듣기도 했지만, 내겐 어느새 첫사랑과도
같은 존재가 되어버린 프라이드였다. 프라이드만 보면
이유 없이 짠해지고 안쓰러운 마음이 드는 날이 많아진
것도 그맘때쯤이었는데, 실제로 어느 폭설이 내린 겨울
날엔 골목길 한켠에 수북이 눈을 맞고 서 있는 프라이
드를 보고 괜스레 찔끔찔끔 눈물을 흘리기도 했다(안타
깝게도 하필 그 모습을 아버지가 또 보고 말았다. 아버지는 내가
눈 내리는 날 차를 밀 생각을 하니, 그게 서러워서 우는 것이라고
여긴 모양이었다. 다음 날, 아버지는 내게 마티즈를 한 대 알아보
라고, 어머니를 통해 말하기도 했다).

나는 다시 한 번, 기아자동차 홍제동 AS센터를 찾았
지만, 그때에도 역시 은색 토시를 한 정비사로부터 '부
품이 없다'는 말만 듣고 돌아서야 했다. 그리고 며칠 동
안 계속 운행을 하지 못한 채, 멀거니 프라이드를 바라

er to tell me to look into the cost of a Matiz.)

I went back to the Kia Motors service center in Hongje-dong but again, the mechanic with the silver work sleeves told me that they couldn't get the parts, so I came back home. For the next few days, I couldn't drive the Pride and I gazed at it vacantly until I suddenly remembered the "Samjeon Automobile Service Center" written in Uncle's notebook. Luckily, their phone number had remained the same.

There were two people working at the Samjeon Automobile Service Center. One was a young guy who went by "Mr. Kim," and the other was a fat man, the boss, who easily looked like he was in his late sixties. As soon as I drove up in the Pride, they said nothing and just took the car keys from me. Then, while I stood there, they both got into the Pride and disappeared in the direction of Sindorim-dong. I didn't know what the hell was going on, so I just stood there, alone in the front yard of the service center, staring in the direction that the Pride had vanished into. I found out later on that this was the unique way the service center ran its diagnostics. Mr. Kim and the fat boss never asked the customer questions. They'd take the car for a

만 보다가, 그러다가 생각해낸 것이 삼촌의 노트 속에 적혀 있던 '삼전자동차공업사'였다. 그곳의 전화번호는 다행히 그때까지도 변하지 않고 있었다.

삼전자동차공업사에는 '김 군'이라고 불리는 청년 한 명과, 얼핏 봐도 육십대 중반은 넘은 것 같은 뚱뚱한 남자 사장 단둘이 근무하고 있었는데, 그들은 내가 프라이드를 몰고 들어서자마자 아무 말 없이 손에서 차 키부터 뺏어 들었다. 그러곤 나를 남겨두고, 둘이 프라이드에 올라타서 신도림동 방향으로 사라졌다. 나는 공업사 앞마당에 혼자 선 채, 이게 대체 무슨 경우인가 당황해서 한참 동안 차가 사라진 방향만 바라보고 서 있었는데, 후에 알고 보니, 그건 그 공업사만의 독특한 수리 절차였다. 김 군과 뚱뚱한 남자 사장은 항상 손님에게 무언가를 묻지 않고, 자신들이 직접 도로를 달려보고 난 후에야 정비를 시작하곤 했다. 내가 찾아간 첫날도 마찬가지였다. 프라이드를 몰고 나간 지 10분 정도 지난 다음 돌아온 그들은, 역시 내게 아무런 말도 하지 않고 주섬주섬 창고 한쪽 벽면에 책장처럼 쌓아 올린 플라스틱 바구니들을 뒤지기 시작했다. 그러곤 브레이크 페달을 하나 찾아와 짧게 물었다.

test drive by themselves before starting any repairs. That's what they were doing the first time I went there. They came back with the Pride about ten minutes later, still saying nothing. They started shuffling through the plastic containers that were stacked on one wall of the warehouse like a bookshelf. Then they both approached me, a brake pedal in the boss's hand, and asked me curtly, "Replacing it, right?"

Still befuddled, I didn't know what to say and just shook my head. While Mr. Kim replaced the brake pedal, the fat boss took the liberty of changing the brake oil.

"Excuse me, but..." I felt a bit intimidated by their silence and couldn't ask my question properly.

"Don't worry, we're just replacing everything that needs to be replaced." The fat boss took short, loud breaths while he siphoned off the old brake oil into a drum can. After listening to his heavy breathing for a bit, I don't know why, but I felt like I could trust them. So, without saying another word, I just stood there and watched them work.

After the repairs were finished, it came out to be less than what I'd expected. As I handed the money over to Mr. Kim, I stopped and asked him, "Hey, do

—갈 거죠?

나는 대답을 제대로 하지 못하고 그저 고개만 끄덕거렸다. 김 군이라는 사람이 브레이크 페달을 교체하는 동안, 뚱뚱한 사장은 역시 내게 허락도 받지 않고 브레이크 오일을 교환했다.

—저기, 저 그건……

나는 그들의 침묵에 조금 주눅이 들어서, 물어볼 말들을 제대로 못 물어보았다.

—다 갈아야 하는 거 가는 거니까. 염려 마쇼.

뚱뚱한 사장은 숨을 씩씩, 거칠게 몰아쉬며 오래된 브레이크 오일을 드럼통에 받아냈다. 나는 그 숨소리를 듣고 난 뒤에야 왠지 모르게 그들에게 신뢰가 생겼고, 그래서 아무 말 없이, 묵묵히 그들의 작업을 지켜보았다.

모든 정비가 다 끝난 후, 예상보다 적게 나온 비용을 김 군에게 건네다 말고, 내가 물었다.

—저기, 혹시 여기선 오토미션 교환은 안 되나요? 이게 후진이 안 돼서…… 거, 무슨 패킹 때문이라고 하던데.

김 군은 아무 말 없이 나를 빤히 바라보다가, 뚱뚱한 사장 쪽을 돌아보았다.

you guys also replace transmissions? My car won't go in reverse. They said there was something wrong with the rubber gasket or something."

Mr. Kim just stared at me then turned to look at the fat boss.

The fat boss had a towel around his neck and he asked me, "Did you buy it used?"

"Pardon me?"

"I'm asking you if you bought this car used."

"Well, not exactly but..."

The boss took a huge gulp of water straight from his water bottle and said, "Whoever drove this car drove it like that from the beginning, so just keep driving it like that."

"Do you know this car?"

"I can't remember people, but I never forget a car."

I took a step closer towards the boss.

"This car didn't go in reverse from the very beginning? They said it was because the rubber gasket had worn out."

"No. I took out the rubber gasket."

"You took it out? Here? On purpose? Why?"

"How am I supposed to know why? I just did as I was asked."

—거, 중고로 사셨수?

뚱뚱한 사장은 목에 수건을 걸친 채, 내게 물었다.

—네?

—거, 중고로 차를 구입했나, 묻는 거요.

—아니, 그런 건 아니지만……

나는 말끝을 흐렸다.

—거, 그 차는 처음부터 그렇게 탔으니까, 그냥 그렇게 알고 타슈.

사장은 생수병을 통째로 들고 마신 후, 그렇게 말했다.

—이 차를 아세요?

—사람은 기억 못 해도, 차는 다 기억하지.

나는 사장 앞으로 한 걸음 더 다가갔다.

—이 차가 원래부터 후진이 안 된 거예요? 무슨 패킹이 떨어져서 그렇다고 하던데……

—그 패킹을 내가 뺐수다.

—여, 여기서요……? 일부러요? 아니, 왜요?

—사정이야 나도 알 수 없지. 나야 그저 해달라고 하니까 해준 거뿐이니까.

나는 사장에게 무언가 더 물어보고 싶었지만, 그러나

I wanted to ask the boss more questions, but I decided not to. For some reason, I felt like that was all he knew.

"But, you know what?"

As he returned the car keys to me, the boss suddenly asked.

"That's the reason why this car is still running. Because it can't go in reverse."

I stared at the boss for a moment, and then managed to ask him what he meant.

"Well think about it. There's less strain on the engine. It's all the extra functions that ruin the actual performance of a car. People just don't know that."

I gave a slight nod and got back into the Pride. The brake pedal felt tight as if it had a spring attached to the bottom of it.

12

I continued driving Uncle's Pride for a long time after that. It ran smoothly without any minor problems and during that time, I entered my Ph.D. program. Grandmother was still in and out of hospital and, at each meal, she had to take a handful of meds. But even so, at nighttime she would always

그러지 않았다. 왠지 그게 전부일 거란 생각이 들었기 때문이었다.

—한데, 그거 아슈?

차 키를 건네받고 돌아서는 나에게 사장이 물었다.

—이 차는 그래서 지금까지 굴러가게 된 거라우. 후진이 안 되니까.

나는 다시 사장의 얼굴을 바라보며, 그건 또 왜 그렇죠, 라고 작은 목소리로 물었다.

—아무래도 엔진에 무리가 덜 가지 않았겠수? 원래 잡다한 기능들 때문에 제 기능들이 망가지는 법이라우. 사람들이 그걸 몰라서 그렇지.

나는 살짝 고개를 끄덕이고, 다시 프라이드에 올라탔다. 브레이크 페달은 마치 뒤에 스프링을 달아놓은 듯, 팽팽하게 움직였다.

12

그 뒤로도 나는 쭉 삼촌의 프라이드를 몰고 다녔다. 프라이드는 잔고장 하나 없이 잘 달려주었고, 그사이 나는 대학원 박사 과정에 진학하게 되었다. 할머니는

poke me in the shoulder and say, "Hey, hey. Are you sleeping?" Auntie sold her apartment and moved in with us but Grandmother stubbornly insisted on sharing a room with me. I joked with Grandmother to stop harassing a grandson who was worth less than a car, but she refused to change rooms. So I was able to continue hearing her stories about Uncle.

I'd also started a relationship with the very same junior that I'd taken to Han River Park. After graduating from college, she went to work at an ad agency. I think it was the seventh or eighth time, but after I kept showing up at her house, she finally gave in and got into the Pride. Then she said, "Seeing you ride this piece of junk for so long, well at least you're not one to fool around." Of course, she said this while giving me a whack on the shoulder. As soon as she finished, I drove the car directly to Han River Park, and unlike the first time, I put the car in neutral, got out of the driver's seat and swiftly parked the car. At that point, just by looking at the empty parking stall, I immediately knew how hard I needed to push, so there was no more making her walk the Han riverside by herself. That day, inside the Pride, I shared my official first

입퇴원을 반복하며 매 끼니마다 한 움큼씩이나 되는 약을 먹고 있었지만, 여전히 한밤중이 되면 '야 야, 자냐?' 하며 내 어깨를 톡톡, 건드렸다. 고모는 살고 있던 아파트를 모두 처분하고 아예 우리 집으로 들어왔지만, 그러나 할머니는 계속 나와 같은 방을 쓰겠다고 고집을 부렸다. 나는 할머니에게 '자동차만도 못한 손주, 그만 좀 괴롭히라'고 말했지만, 그러나 방을 옮기지는 않았다. 그래서 나는 할머니에게 계속 삼촌의 이야기를 들을 수 있게 되었다.

그사이 나는 연애도 하게 되었는데, 상대는 예전 한강시민공원에 함께 갔던 바로 그 여자 후배였다. 후배는 그동안 학교를 졸업하고 광고대행사에 취직을 했는데, 일곱 번째인가 여덟 번째인가, 내가 계속 집 앞으로 찾아가자 못 이기는 척 프라이드에 올라탔다. 그러면서 후배는 내게 '똥차를 오래 타고 다니는 걸 보니까 그래도 뭐, 딴짓은 안 하겠네'라고 말했다. 물론 내 어깨를 한번 퉁, 치면서 한 말이었다. 나는 후배의 말이 끝나자마자 곧장 한강시민공원으로 차를 몰고 갔다. 그리고 예전과는 달리, 기어를 중립에 놓고 운전석에서 내려 신속하게 주차를 마쳤다. 그땐 이미 빈자리를 한번 쓱

kiss with her.

After starting my relationship with her, I actually spent even more time alone in the Pride. My girlfriend's company was famous for working its employees overtime, as if it was a part of their very mission statement, and all the employees, except for the president, faithfully carried out their duties. I felt bad for her so I would park the car in front of her building and wait for however long it took for her to finish. Usually, I'd turn on the interior light and read a book while waiting. But sometimes, I'd tilt the driver's seat all the way back and just lie there.

Lying there like that, I'd sometimes think of Uncle. Over the years, I thought that I'd heard a lot of stories and discovered quite a bit about Uncle and his Pride. But, for some reason, I still felt like I was stuck at square one with him. The moment when I thought I'd figured it out, Uncle again felt like he was just out of reaching distance, and the moment when I felt like I had almost matched all the pieces of the puzzle, I'd suddenly find a new piece that would mess it all up again. So I readily accepted the conclusion that what I already knew about him was all the information I'd ever get. That the only

바라만 봐도, 어느 정도 세기로 밀어야 하는지 답이 나올 정도였으니, 후배 혼자 한강변을 돌아다니게 하는 일은 만들지 않았다. 나는 그날 후배와 프라이드 안에서 정식으로, 첫 키스를 하기도 했다.

연애를 시작하고 난 뒤, 나는 이전보다 프라이드에 혼자 앉아 있는 시간이 더 늘어났다. 후배의 회사는 야근을 무슨 사훈쯤으로 여기고 사장 이하 전 직원이 충실히 실천하는 직장으로도 유명했는데, 나는 그게 좀 안타까워 종종 차를 대고 그 앞에서 무작정 기다리는 일을 반복했다. 대개는 실내등을 켜놓고 책을 읽으면서 후배를 기다렸지만, 때로는 운전석을 최대한 뒤로 젖히고 가만히 누워 있기도 했다. 그러면서 나는 가끔씩 삼촌 생각을 하기도 했다. 그때까지 나는 삼촌에 대해서, 또한 프라이드에 대해서, 많은 이야기를 듣고, 또 많은 것을 알게 되었다고 생각했지만, 그래도 모든 건 제자리에 멈춰 있는 듯한 기분이 들었다. 조금 알게 되었다고 생각하는 순간, 삼촌은 다시 저만큼 달아났고, 무언가 흩어진 퍼즐을 거의 다 맞췄다고 생각한 순간, 또 다른 모양의 조각이 튀어나와 그림을 한순간에 원점으로

thing I could do now was to go over the stories, over and over and over again.

Of course, these were all thoughts I had while I sat in the Pride. I wondered, if I hadn't driven Uncle's Pride, then would I have thought this much about Uncle? But honestly, I wasn't so sure. On the contrary, I was a little worried. I was scared that one day, Uncle would come back unannounced. That he would take the car back from me. The Pride was now registered in my name (the papers in the glove compartment were documents you needed to scrap a car, but they were also the same documents needed to change ownership), but I would sometimes picture this happening, and whenever I did, I'd feel a bit lonely...

But all of these thoughts disappeared after I uncovered even more hidden secrets between Uncle and the Pride, which even led me to take a trip down to Hadong. After that, whenever I lay in the Pride with my eyes closed, the only thoughts that would come to mind were the roads that the Pride had traveled on and the paths that the Pride had taken. Because when doing that, my body would become numb, but sometimes, it would also begin to heat up.

만들어놓았다. 그래서 나는 그것이 내가 알 수 있는, 삼촌의 거의 모든 이야기가 아닐까, 이제 내가 할 수 있는 일은 그저 알고 있는 이야기들을 반복하고, 반복하고, 또 반복하는 일이 아닐까, 지레짐작 손쉽게 생각해버리기도 했다. 물론 그것들은 모두 내가 프라이드에 앉아서 한 생각들이기도 했다. 나는 만약 삼촌의 프라이드를 몰지 않았다면, 내가 이만큼이나 삼촌에 대한 생각을 하게 되었을까 의심해보았는데, 솔직히 그 부분에 대해선 자신이 없었다. 반대로 나는 어떤 편이었는가하면, 어느 날 삼촌이 예고도 하지 않은 채 돌아올까봐, 그래서 내게서 다시 프라이드를 찾아갈까봐, 염려하고 있는 편이 맞았다. 이미 내 앞으로 명의 이전도 해둔 프라이드였지만(콘솔박스에서 발견한 삼촌의 서류들은, 폐차에 필요한 서류들이기도 했지만, 명의 이전을 할 때도 똑같이 쓰이는 서류들이었다), 나는 종종 그런 상상을 했고, 그때마다 조금씩 쓸쓸해지기도 했다……

하지만, 그런 모든 생각들은, 이후 내가 삼촌과 프라이드의 숨겨진 어떤 이야기들을 새롭게 알게 되면서, 또 그것 때문에 하동까지 한번 내려갔다가 올라온 다음부터 모두 사라지게 되었는데, 그 뒤로는 그저 가만히

13

Up until that point, the one person that I hadn't factored in was Auntie's ex-husband. Why didn't I think of him sooner? While I was driving down to Hadong, I briefly blamed myself over something I was blameless of because it was natural, only natural, that I didn't think of him. In every story, people always leave blanks, and in order to fill these blanks, they create different stories. That's the origin of how all stories are born but up until then, I wasn't aware of this. Just looking at Auntie's ex-husband, I realized this. Whether it was conscious or unconscious, the reason why I refused to think about him until then was probably because to me, *that* story was a blank—a story that I didn't want to discuss...

He'd started hitting Auntie as soon as they'd gotten married. Usually, he beat her when he got drunk, and Auntie ended up being hospitalized twice and also suffered from tinnitus. A couple of times, Father got involved and tried to get them divorced, but he failed every time because Auntie refused. When Auntie finally did decide to get a di-

두 눈을 감고 프라이드가 달려온 길들을, 달려왔던 길들만 떠올리게 되었다. 그것만으로도 가슴이 먹먹하게, 때론 뜨겁게 달아올랐기 때문이었다.

13

그러니까 그때까지도 미처 내가 생각하지 못하고 있던 사람은 바로 고모부였다. 왜 그 생각을 미리 못 했을까. 하동에 내려가는 차 안에서 나는 짧게 자책 아닌 자책을 했지만, 또 한편으론 그게 당연하다는, 당연했다는 마음이 들기도 했다. 사람들은 저마다 이야기 속에 한 가지씩 여백을 두고, 그 여백을 채우려 다른 이야기들을 만들어내는 법인데, 그게 이 세상 모든 이야기들이 태어나는 자리인데, 그때의 나는 그것을 미처 알지 못하고 있었던 것이다. 고모부만 해도 그렇다. 내가 고모부에 대해서 의식적으로든 무의식적으로든 생각하지 않으려 했던 것은, 아마 그 부분이 내겐 여백과도 같은 부분이었기 때문일 것이다. 말하고 싶지 않은 이야기 같은 것……

고모부는 결혼 초기부터 고모를 때렸다. 주로 술만 마

vorce, it was after a long period of time had passed. It wasn't his abuse but rather his affair that finally convinced her. Apparently, Auntie's ex-husband had hooked up a few times with a female officer who worked in the traffic patrol department at the same police precinct. When Auntie found out about this, she signed the divorce papers without any hesitation. The reason why Auntie was so resolute in her decision was because she saw the black and blue bruises around the female officer's left eye. That day, she hugged Grandmother tightly and began to sob, saying that nothing made her sadder than seeing that. Well, whatever the case, Auntie's ex-husband was henceforth referred to as "that piece of shit" and "the scum of the earth" by our family. So naturally, I avoided him and so wasn't able to think about him.

Now that I think about it, perhaps all of this was the fate of this story. But if, at that junction, if Auntie hadn't asked me to drop off some kimchi to my cousins, and if I hadn't found her ex-husband sitting alone in the living room drinking *soju*, then this story might have had a very different cast to it and the conclusion might have gone down a very different path. If this story was written solely about

시면 손찌검을 해댔는데, 그것 때문에 고모는 병원에 두 번 입원하기도 했고, 따로 이명을 앓기도 했다. 아버지는 몇 번 나서서 두 사람을 이혼시키려 했지만, 번번이 고모의 반대로 무산되었다. 정작 고모가 이혼을 결심한 것은 그 후로도 꽤 오랜 시간이 지난 다음의 일이었는데, 손찌검이 아닌 고모부의 외도가 결정적인 사유가 되었다. 고모부는 그때 같은 경찰서 교통계에 근무하고 있던 여경과 몇 번 따로 만난 모양이었는데, 그 사실을 알게 된 고모는 단 한순간도 망설이지 않고 이혼 서류에 도장을 찍어버렸다. 고모가 그렇게 단호하게 결정을 내리게 된 것은 여경의 왼쪽 눈 주위에 시퍼렇게 나 있던 멍을 보았기 때문이었는데, 그걸 보는 순간 그렇게 서러울 수가 없었다고, 고모는 할머니 품에 안겨 엉엉 울기도 했다. 어쨌든, 그 일로 인해 고모부는 우리 집에서 주로 '쓰레기만도 못한 위인' '인간 말종'쯤으로 불리게 되었고, 그로 인해 나 역시도 자연스럽게 고모부를 피하고, 생각하지 못하게 된 것이었다.

생각해보면 그 또한 다 이 이야기의 운명이었을지 모르지만, 만약 그때 내가 고모의 심부름으로 사촌들에게 김치를 가져다주러 가지 않았다면, 그리고 만약 그때

the Pride, then everything about Uncle would have remained a blank and the story would still be driving in circles around Han River Park. But the fact that it wasn't is the fate of this story. Now the time to fill in the blanks has come. Twenty-three—blank one. The man that Auntie had fallen in love with was her now ex-husband. Blank two. Even then, he was a police officer. These are the blanks.

The reason Auntie's ex-husband told me the story was of course, because of the Pride. I told him that I didn't need his help, but he insisted and came down to the apartment parking lot, helped me take the kimchi out from the trunk of the Pride, and carried it with me to the elevator. Then quickly turning around, he looked at the Pride and said, "It's sickening when you think about how long that car's been running."

I still felt uncomfortable being around him so I laughed once, awkwardly, and said that for an '87 model, it was still running great.

"Oh, I know. I know it's an '87 model. 300,000 *won* of my money went into paying for it."

As he said this, he looked at the Pride one more time. The reason why I stayed that day, ate kimchi and drank *soju* with Auntie's abusive ex-husband,

고모부가 혼자 마루에 앉아 소주를 마시고 있지 않았다면, 이 이야기는 전혀 다른 방향으로, 전혀 다른 색깔로 마무리되었을지 모를 일이다. 그랬다면, 이 이야기는 어쩌면 프라이드를 위해, 삼촌의 이야기를 모두 여백으로 돌리고, 계속 한강시민공원 주위를 맴돌았을지도 모를 일이다. 하지만 그럴 수 없었던 것이 바로 이 이야기의 운명이다. 이제 그 여백을 채워야 하는 순간이 온 것이다. 스물세 살, 당시 고모가 사랑에 빠졌던 사람이 바로 고모부였다는 사실, 그때도 고모부는 경찰관이었다는 사실. 바로 그 여백 말이다.

고모부가 나에게 그 이야기를 꺼내게 된 것은 역시 프라이드 때문이었다. 그러지 않아도 된다고 했지만, 고모부는 굳이 아파트 주차장까지 내려와, 나와 함께 프라이드 트렁크에 실려 있던 김치통을 엘리베이터로 날랐다. 그러면서 획, 프라이드를 돌아보면서 말했다.

—저놈도 징글징글하게 오래 달리는구나.

나는 그때까지도 고모부에게 무언가 좀 어색한 기분이 남아 있어, 슬쩍 웃으면서 87년산인데 아직도 저렇게 쌩쌩해요, 라고 말해주었다.

was because of this last comment.

14

Back in '87, the Guro-dong Worker's Labor Union that Uncle belonged to was actually under police surveillance after it became the main target of an investigation by the public security division of the district police precinct. They fell under such heavy surveillance because key members of the group were all laborers with college backgrounds. After 1985, there was a growing number of cases where college graduates were entering various companies under false pretenses, claiming to need work experience. It was a huge headache for both the investigators and the company owners. But the company owners were somewhat in a better position because back then, it was illegal to establish multiple labor unions in one workplace. So the owners, as a preemptive strategy, placed their own people, those who were about to be promoted to managerial positions, in the only existing labor union leader positions.

But that's what made the investigators' jobs even more difficult. Because these laborers with college

—나도 잘 알지, 87년산이라는 걸. 저놈 살 때 내 돈도 30만 원이나 들어갔는데, 뭘.

고모부는 그러면서 다시 한 번 프라이드를 돌아다보았다. 그러니까 그날 내가 고모부와 함께, 고모가 싸준 김치를 안주 삼아 소주를 마시게 된 건, 바로 그 말 때문이었다.

14

87년 당시, 삼촌이 가입해 있던 구로동일꾼노동자회는 사실 관할 경찰서 공안계로부터 요 사찰 대상으로 분류돼, 집중 감시를 받고 있던 처지였다. 이유는 그 모임의 주축 멤버들이 대부분 '학출(學出)'들로 이루어져 있었기 때문이었다. 85년 이후부터 현장 실천을 내세우고 각 사업장마다 대학 졸업생들이 위장 취업을 하는 일들이 빈번히 발생했는데, 그 때문에 사업주나 관할 경찰서 형사들은 골머리를 썩어야만 했다. 그나마 사업주의 입장은 좀 나은 편이었던 게, 그때는 아직 복수 노조가 허용되지 않던 시절인지라 대부분 노조 집행부 인원들을 주임 승진 대상자나 반장 출신들로 미리 채워놓

backgrounds couldn't legally organize democratic labor unions, they rallied the regional laborers to voluntarily establish gatherings, and within these gatherings, they carried out educational programs centered on cultivating cultural movements and social consciousness. The investigators had to target not only all levels of businesses, but had to expand the scope of their investigations to cover the entire area of Guro-dong. So during that time, the twenty or so investigators in the public safety division at the Yeongdeungpo police precinct were separated into groups and each group was assigned to track a specific gathering. The gathering that Auntie's ex-husband was placed in charge of was the Guro-dong Worker's Labor Union.

"Honestly, when I first met your aunt, it's true that I purposely met her for the sake of the investigation. Your aunt was the youngest in the group and she had been working at the factory for the shortest length of time. But above everything else, she had never gone to college. Eager to crack the case, I deliberately approached your aunt. Of course it wasn't like that after... Even now, your aunt probably doesn't know exactly what role she played."

He told me that he had approached Auntie by

을 수 있었기 때문이었다. 형사들이 바빠진 건 오히려 그 때문이기도 했다. 합법적 민주 노조를 세울 수 없게 된 학출들은 그 대신 지역 노동자들의 자발적인 모임을 설립, 그 안에서 문화운동과 의식 교육운동을 병행해나 갔는데, 그로 인해 형사들의 감시 대상은 각 단위 사업 장뿐만 아니라 구로동 전체로 퍼져나갔기 때문이었다. 해서 당시 스무 명이 넘던 영등포경찰서 공안계 형사들 은 각각 팀을 나눠 몇몇 모임들의 뒤를 밟았는데, 그때 고모부가 담당했던 모임이 바로 구로동일꾼노동자회 였다.

　—솔직히 그때 네 고모를 처음 만난 건…… 일 때문 에 의도적으로 만난 게 맞아. 네 고모가 나이도 제일 어 렸고, 공장 경력도 제일 짧았고, 무엇보다 학출도 아니 었으니까. 일 욕심에 일부러 다가간 거지…… 물론 그 다음엔 그렇지 않았지만…… 그래서 네 고모는 지금도 자기가 무슨 일을 한 건지 모르고 있는 거야……

　고모부는 그때 자신을 은행원으로 속이고 고모에게 접근했다고 한다. 보다 철저하게 일을 진행시키기 위해 고모 명의의 통장도 개설해주고, 거기에 한 번에 몇 십 만 원씩 입금을 해주기도 했다. 고모에겐 은행에서 발

disguising himself as a bank clerk. To be completely thorough in his role, he had even opened up a bank account in her name and made a lump sum deposit of a few hundred thousand *won*. He explained to her that the money was from slush funds connected to the bank, but it was actually the money he'd secretly saved by skimming the expense and activity allowance allotted for his investigations. Believing he was a competent, polite bank clerk, Auntie immediately fell in love. After that, even if he didn't ask her, Auntie started telling him everything that was going on each day.

Thanks to her, he was able to easily figure out information such as where the leaflets they used at the gatherings were generally printed, what factories the group members were affiliated with, and roughly how much it cost to operate their meetings. He even had a plan all set up to arrest them under charges of violation of the national security laws and was waiting for an opportunity to go in, but out of nowhere, someone brought in an assault charge first. The victim was Uncle, and the assailant was...almost all of the members of the labor group.

"That caught me by surprise. Your uncle was accused of being a snitch. Turns out the members

생하는 비자금이라고 설명했지만, 사실 그건 고모부가 활동비와 업무수당비를 따로 모아, 남몰래 저축해둔 돈 이기도 했다. 고모부를 실력 있고 예의 바른 은행원으로 여긴 고모는 금세 사랑에 빠지게 되었고, 그다음부 턴 고모부가 따로 묻지 않아도 재잘재잘, 그날그날 있 었던 일들을 남김없이 늘어놓기 시작한 것이었다.

덕분에 고모부는 모임에 쓰이는 책자들이 주로 어디에서 인쇄되는지, 모임의 구성원들이 어느 어느 공장에 속해 있는지, 모임에 드는 경비는 어느 정도인지, 손쉽 게 파악할 수 있었다. 그리고 기회를 틈타 모두 국가보 안법 위반 혐의로 검거할 계획까지 세웠는데, 엉뚱하게도 폭행사건이 먼저 일어난 것이었다. 피해자는 삼촌이 었고, 가해자에는 모임 대부분의 인원들이 포함된……

―사실 그건 나도 좀 의외였는데…… 네 삼촌이 모임 내에서 프락치로 몰린 모양이더라구. 알고 봤더니 그때 그 사람들도 자꾸 정보가 새어 나가니까, 이상하다, 이 상하다, 속으로만 생각을 하고 있었는데, 거기에, 네 삼 촌이 바로 저 차, 저 프라이드를 몰고 나타난 거야. 그때 당시 네 삼촌이나 네 고모나 모두 일당제로 월급을 받 고 있었거든. 네 삼촌 하루 일당이 아마 8천9백 원쯤 됐

were all thinking that it was strange because their information kept getting leaked, and that's when your uncle showed up with that car, the Pride. Back then, your aunt and uncle were both getting by on daily wages, and your uncle was probably only being paid around 8,900 *won* per day. After paying the rent and taking off this and that tax, he would've been left with practically nothing. But then for a person like that to suddenly show up with a Pride that cost around a few million *won*? Of course they got suspicious. And that's probably what led to the beating."

At first, the people in the group probably jokingly asked him where he'd gotten the car. But there was no way Uncle would've answered them honestly. There was no way that he was going to tell them that his mom had bought him the car so he could cart around women, because the girl he liked would've heard it as well.

"Well regardless, as I investigated the assault charge, I was able to arrest the remaining people. It was the perfect scenario since the foul leftist powers had now resorted to violence. It was better than we could've ever imagined. The only problem was your uncle. His name was definitely on the

을 거야. 자취방 월세 내고, 이런저런 세금 떼고 나면 아무것도 손에 쥘 수 없는 돈이었지. 한데, 그런 사람이 갑자기 몇 백만 원짜리 프라이드를 몰고 나타나니 의심을 받을 수밖에. 아마 그러다가 린치사건으로 이어진 모양이야……

어쩌면 그때 당시 같은 모임에 있던 사람들은 삼촌에게 웬 자동차냐고, 처음엔 웃으면서 물어봤을지도 모를 일이다. 하지만 삼촌은 말을 제대로 하지 못했을 것이 분명하다. 우리 엄마가 여자 태워주라고 사준 거예요, 삼촌은 그 말을 차마 하진 못했을 것이다. 그 자리엔 그 여자 또한 분명 함께 있었을 테니까……

—어쨌든 그 사건 조사하면서 나머지 사람들도 모두 구속할 수 있었지. 모양새가 좋잖아. 불순좌경세력들이 폭력까지 휘둘렀으니까, 우리가 예상한 그림보다 훨씬 좋은 그림이 나온 거야. 문제는…… 네 삼촌이었는데, 분명 모임엔 이름이 올라가 있으니까 기소를 하는 게 마땅한데, 그러기엔 내가 좀 미안한 거야. 그래서 내가 우리 반장한테 사실 저 친군 빨대가 맞다고, 내가 활동비로 따로 포섭한 친구라고 말해준 거지. 그 말도 아주 틀린 건 아니었던 게 그 프라이드를 살 때 내가 네 고모

member register, so it was only right to arrest him. But to do that, I felt sorry towards him. So I told my chief that he was actually my informant. That I had paid him and had brought him in to work for me. And that wasn't completely a lie since the money that I had deposited under your aunt's name, the 300,000 *won*, had gone into buying the Pride. Of course, your aunt had said that she was just borrowing it for a bit..."

"Uncle. Did Uncle know about this?" I downed my shot of *soju*.

"Of course. I told him while he was on his way out after the investigation had finished. Back then, 300,000 *won* was a lot of money."

It was then that I understood why the Pride didn't go in reverse; I felt like I had finally solved the puzzle. I knew that it had something to do with the 300,000 *won*.

"I heard that among the members there was a girl that Uncle liked. Do you know her?"

"Know her? Of course. She was one of the group's leaders so I personally wrote up the report on her. She was sentenced to jail time and when she got out a year later, she immediately left for Cheongju. I'm pretty sure your Uncle came to see me some-

명의로 넣어둔 돈 중에서 30만 원이 빠져나갔거든. 물론 네 고모는 그때 잠깐 빌려 쓴다고 생각했겠지만 말이야……

—삼촌도, 삼촌도 그걸 알게 되었나요?

나는 술잔을 단숨에 입 안에 털어 넣으며 물었다.

—그럼, 잘 알지. 네 삼촌 조사 끝나고 나갈 때 내가 다 말해줬으니까. 그때 30만 원이면 꽤 큰돈이었거든.

나는 그제야 프라이드가 후진되지 않는 이유를, 그 수수께끼를 푼 것만 같은 기분이 들었다. 어쩌면, 어쩌면, 그것은 그 30만 원과 관계된 일일지도 몰랐다.

—거기에 삼촌이 좋아했던 여자도 한 명 있었다던데…… 혹시, 모르세요?

—모르긴, 잘 알지. 주동급이어서 내가 직접 조서 꾸몄는걸…… 걘, 그때 형기 받고 그다음 해에 바로 청주로 갔지, 아마. 네 삼촌도 그 뒤에 나한테 찾아와서 걔 어디로 갔냐고 물어본 적이 있었어……

15

고모부가 알아봐준 여자의 정확한 주소는 경남 하동

124

time after to ask me where she'd gone."

15

The girl's exact address that Auntie's ex-husband looked up for me was Beopwang-li Hwagae-eup, in Hadong-gun, Gyeongsangnam-do. If you passed Ssanggyesa Temple and traveled on a small road for about ten kilometers in the direction of Chilbulsa Temple, then you'd reach her place, her hometown.

At first, when I departed Seoul for Hadong, I thought that maybe I'd find Uncle there. So before my departure, I put two copies of my resident registration papers and authentication certificate of personal seal inside the glove compartment of the Pride. If I did meet Uncle, I was just going to leave the Pride there, just like Uncle had done. But when the Pride and I began to near Nonsan, I thought that I wouldn't find Uncle there, and decided instead that I would just meet the girl and ask her a few questions. But then when I passed the Gokseong tollgate and started heading in the direction of Gurye, I thought, no, let's not. Let's just travel the same path that the Pride had previously traveled.

군 화개읍 법왕리로 되어 있었다. 쌍계사를 지나 칠불사 방향으로 작은 도로를 타고 10킬로미터쯤 올라가면, 거기가 바로 여자가 살고 있는, 여자의 고향이었다.

처음, 서울에서 하동으로 출발할 때쯤만 해도, 나는 어쩌면 거기에 삼촌이 있을지도 모른다고 생각했다. 그래서 프라이드 콘솔박스에 내 인감증명서와 주민등록초본을 각각 두 통씩 넣어두고 출발했다. 삼촌을 만나면, 나는 거기에 그냥 프라이드를 놓아두고 올 생각이었다. 예전, 삼촌이 한 방식 그대로…… 하지만, 프라이드가 논산 근처에 접어들었을 때, 나는 삼촌이 그곳에 없을지도 모른다는 생각을 하게 됐고, 그냥 그 여자를 만나 이런저런 얘기나 듣고 오자, 마음을 고쳐먹었다. 그러나 또 차가 곡성 톨게이트를 지나 구례 방향으로 접어들었을 땐, 그러지도 말자, 그냥 프라이드가 갔던 길을 한번 똑같이 따라갔다가 되돌아오자,로 바뀌게 되었고, 그 결심은 쌍계사를 지날 때까지도 변하지 않게 되었다.

때는 또 벚꽃이 피는 4월이었던지라, 나는 쌍계사 입

My mind had changed once again and this final thought remained until I passed by Ssanggyesa Temple.

It happened to be April when the cherry blossoms were in full bloom. It was less than five kilometers from the entrance to Ssanggyesa Temple to the parking lot, but it took a whole two hours to finally pass through the area. The cars moved slowly along the one way tunnel made by the overhanging cherry blossom trees, allowing the flower petals sufficient time to fall. Occasionally, the cherry blossoms cast a great shadow over the entire road and so the falling petals stood out all the more brilliantly, and landed on the Pride's windshield in stark relief of the scene outside. I got out of the car for a few minutes and snapped a picture of the Pride with my cell phone, blanketed by the cherry blossom petals. But then I immediately erased it. For some reason, it reminded me of a funeral bier, as if the Pride was making its final goodbyes.

The girl's house was located in the Chilbulsa Valley, next to a small trail that hikers used to hike up Jiri Mountain. It was a three-room *hanok* built next to a slope, and it looked a bit unstable. It seemed like it was doubling as a B&B and a restaurant that

구에서부터 쌍계사 주차장까지 채 5킬로미터도 되지 않는 거리를 무려 두 시간이나 걸린 다음에야 겨우 지나칠 수가 있었다. 차들은 벚나무로 터널을 이룬 일방통행로를 천천히, 꽃잎이 휘날리는 것을 충분히 기다려주면서 움직였다. 때때로 도로는 벚꽃 그늘을 만나 잠깐잠깐씩 어두워지기도 했는데, 그래서 꽃잎들은 더 환해졌고, 더 선명하게 차 유리창 위로 떨어졌다. 나는 잠깐 차에서 내려, 벚꽃들이 우수수 달라붙어 있는 프라이드를 휴대전화 카메라에 담았는데, 그러나 이내 지워버리고 말았다. 어쩐지 꼭 상여 같다는, 이별의 수순 같다는 느낌이 들었기 때문이었다.

여자의 집은 칠불사 계곡에 위치한, 지리산 등산객들을 위한 작은 탐방로 옆에 있었다. 비탈 바로 옆에, 조금 아슬아슬한 느낌마저 들게 지어진 세 칸짜리 한옥집이 있었는데, 민박도 하고 재첩국을 파는 식당도 겸하고 있는 모양이었다. 그럴 마음도 없었지만, 차가 올라가기엔 좀 무리인 도로인 것 같아, 나는 그냥 여자의 집이 잘 보이는 작은 상회 앞에 프라이드를 대고 한참 동안 운전석에 앉아 있었다. 저녁 무렵이라 여자의 집 굴뚝 위

sold *Jaecheop*-soup. It's not like I had any intention of doing so, but the road leading up to the girl's house seemed unfit for cars so I parked the Pride in front of a shop where I could clearly see the girl's house and just sat there. It was almost evening and I could see white smoke wafting out from the chimney, but there was no sign of people. I watched the smoke curl and rise and finished smoking two more cigarettes before starting the engine to make my way back home.

It was right then that somebody knocked on my window. There were two young girls standing there, dressed in uniforms and carrying backpacks. They looked like they were in middle school.

"Hey mister, this is the car that can't go backwards, right? Right?"

The girl with her hair tied tightly in a ponytail asked. I turned off the engine.

"It is. But, how'd you know that?"

The girls didn't answer my question and started going around in a circle. The ponytailed girl said, "Hurry up and give me my 500 *won*. Come on, hurry up." I got out of the driver's seat and watched them for a while. I wanted to just give her the 500 *won* myself, but then I wasn't really in the mood to

로 하얀 연기가 피어올랐지만, 그러나 사람의 모습은 보이지 않았다. 나는 그 연기를 보면서 두 개비의 담배를 더 피운 다음, 돌아가기 위해 시동을 걸었다.

그때, 누군가 톡톡, 창문을 두들겼다. 교복을 입고 책가방을 멘, 중학생쯤 되어 보이는 소녀들이 두 명 서 있었다.

—아저씨, 아저씨, 이거 뒤로 못 가는 차 맞죠? 그렇죠?

머리를 질끈 하나로 묶은 소녀가 물었다. 나는 다시 시동을 껐다.

—그렇긴 한데…… 넌, 그걸 어떻게 아니?

소녀들은 내 질문엔 대답하지 않고, 거봐, 빨리 5백 원 내놔, 빨리 줘, 하면서 같은 자리를 뱅뱅 맴돌았다. 나는 운전석 밖으로 나와 한참 동안 그런 소녀들을 지켜보았다. 생각 같아선 내가 그냥 5백 원을 주고 싶었지만, 또 그럴 기분은 아니었다.

—전, 그 차 타봤거든요. 어, 그런데 아저씨가 바뀌었네?

소녀는 결국 5백 원을 받지 못한 채 쌕쌕, 숨을 내쉬며 다시 내 앞에 섰다. 5백 원을 주지 않은 소녀는 멀리

either.

"I've been in this car before. Oh, but you're not the same mister."

In the end, she didn't get her 500 *won* and stood in front of me huffing and puffing. The girl who wouldn't give her the 500 *won* was already running away.

"You've been in this car before? When?"

"About three years ago? Once on my way to school and once on my way back home. Now that you mention it..." She paused and began giggling while looking at my Pride.

I cocked my head around towards the Pride and asked, "Why? Is there something wrong with the car?"

"No, it's not that. Just, you'll probably have a hell of a time as well. You see, there's no place to turn the car around here. You have to go all the way to the bottom, but to do that..."

As she said this, the girl let out a big laugh.

"Can't I turn the car around up there?"

"That's only a hiking trail. It gets narrower up there. The mister who used to drive this car had a hell of a time after he drove it all the way up there."

"Up there? To that *hanok* over there?" I pointed to

뛰어가고 있었다.

─이 차를 타봤어? 언제?

─한 3년쯤 됐나? 학교 갈 때 한 번, 집에 올 때 한 번 타봤어요. 어, 그러고 보니……

소녀는 말을 하다 말고 프라이드를 보며 깔깔, 웃어댔다.

─왜 그래? 차에 뭐 묻었니?

나는 고개를 숙여 프라이드를 둘러보면서 물었다.

─아니요, 그게 아니고 아저씨도 고생 좀 하시겠다고요. 여긴 차 돌릴 데가 없거든요. 저 아래까지 내려가야 겨우 돌릴 수 있는데, 그러자면……

소녀는 그렇게 말하면서 또 한 번 크게 웃었다.

─저 위로 가면 돌릴 데가 없니?

─저기는 그냥 등산로예요. 여기보다 길이 더 좁아져요. 예전에 이거 몰던 아저씨도 저 위까지 올라갔다가 엄청 고생한 적 있거든요.

─저 위? 저기 저 한옥집?

나는 손가락으로 여자의 집을 가리키며 물었다.

─네, 저기가 내 친구네 집인데, 언젠가 한번 그 아저씨가 나랑 친구랑 집까지 다 태워준 적이 있었어요.

the house as I asked this.

"Yep. That's my friend's house. That one time, the mister gave me and my friend a ride up to her house."

"Does your friend still live there?" I asked. My throat tightened a little.

Then the girl's expression changed to one that looked a bit mad.

"You just saw her. That loser who ran off with my 500 *won*."

16

The day Uncle's Pride finally stopped running was two years ago, at the end of June. I was worried because the rainy season had been going on for a while and well, wouldn't you know it, the engine wouldn't start. I thought that the battery might have died so I tried a couple of times to restart the car with jumper cables, but it only made grinding noises and the engine wouldn't start. I thought about calling a tow truck and taking it to Samjeon Automobile Service Center, but I decided not to. The Pride had already traveled so far. I just left the Pride parked next to the wall by our house, giving

―네 친구가 저 집에 사니?

나는 조금 작은 목소리로 소녀에게 다시 물었다. 그러자 소녀가 화난 듯한 표정을 지으며 대답했다.

―아저씨도 좀 전에 보셨잖아요? 아까 그 5백 원 갖고 튄 년.

16

삼촌의 프라이드가 완전히 멈춰 선 것은 재작년 6월 말의 일이었다. 장마가 좀 길어져서 걱정을 했더니, 역시나 시동이 걸리지 않았다. 배터리가 방전된 줄 알고 점프 케이블로 몇 번 시도해보았지만, 계속 쉿소리만 낼 뿐, 시동은 걸리지 않았다. 레커차를 불러 삼전자동차공업사까지 갈까도 했지만, 그러나 나는 그러지 않기로 했다. 이미 너무 오랜 길을 달려온 프라이드라는 생각이 들었기 때문이었다. 나는 그냥 계속 프라이드를 담벼락 옆에 세워두기만 했다. 집에 들어올 때나 나갈 때, 통통, 지붕을 두 번씩 두들겨주면서.

내가 다시 그 프라이드를 본 것은, 그러니까 마지막으

it a pat on the hood whenever I left or came back home.

The next time I drove the Pride, which was also the last time that I drove it, was in early October of that year. I was on my way back after taking Grandmother to the hospital when I suddenly pushed the Pride out from behind Father's Sonata. And then, sitting Grandmother down in the passenger seat, I pushed the hood of the car with two hands and went for a spin around the neighborhood. Just once, before the Pride was gone, it's what I wanted to do.

As I pushed the car I asked Grandmother, "Grandmother, do you still like the car better than your own grandson?"

Grandmother didn't give me a reply and just sat there with her back against the passenger seat. She let out a few dry coughs. Then, she finally spoke.

"Hey, hey. Sitting here like this reminds me of long time ago. Back then, your Uncle would push me in the pushcart like this on our way home after finishing work in the fields. He wouldn't pull it. He'd always push it from the back, looking at my face.

I bent down a bit lower and pushed the Pride, trying not to look at Grandmother's face. And then

로 몬 것은 그해 10월 초순의 일이었다. 나는 할머니를 모시고 병원에 다녀오다 말고, 끙끙 아버지의 소나타 뒤에서 프라이드를 빼냈다. 그리고 거기, 조수석에 할머니를 태운 채 보닛을 두 손으로 밀면서 동네 한 바퀴를 돌았다. 그냥 꼭 한 번, 프라이드가 사라지기 전에, 그래 보고 싶었다.

나는 차를 밀면서 할머니한테 물었다.

—할머니, 아직도 손주보다 자동차가 더 좋아?

할머니는 내 질문엔 대답하지 않고, 가만히 조수석 등받이에 기대앉아 있었다. 할머니는 몇 번 마른기침을 하기도 했다. 그러곤 한참 후에 이런 말을 했다.

—야, 야, 이러니까 꼭 옛날 생각난다. 옛날에 네 삼촌도 나랑 논일 끝내고 집으로 돌아올 때면 꼭 리어카를 이렇게 밀었거든. 끌지 않고, 꼭 뒤에서 밀었어. 이 할미 얼굴 계속 바라보면서 말이야……

나는 허리를 더 아래로 깊숙이 숙인 채, 프라이드를 밀었다. 나는 할머니의 얼굴을 보지 않으려고 노력했다. 그러면서 또 생각했다. 삼촌은 이렇게 직접 민 것 또한 노트에 적어놓은 것일까, 그렇다면 그 거리는 과연

a thought occurred to me. Did Uncle also write down the times when he'd pushed the car like this? If so, then how would you calculate the total distance he'd traveled?

Translated by Teresa Kim

어떻게 잴 수 있는 것일까.

『김 박사는 누구인가?』, 문학과지성사, 2013

해설

Afterword

여백, 이야기가 태어나는 자리

정은경 (문학평론가)

「밀수록 다시 가까워지는」은 퍼즐 같은 소설이다. 작가는 몇 개의 단편적인 풍경 조각들을 던져놓고 그 주변의 여백들을 탐정처럼 채워나가면서, 이 모종의 흥미로운 작업에 독자들을 능동적으로 끌어들인다. 어떤 풍경들인가?

  a. 2004년 4월 6일 삼촌은 '프라이드'[1]를 우리 집 담벼락에 주차해놓고 영영 사라졌다.

  b. 삼촌의 프라이드는 1987년 할머니가 장가 못 간 아

---

1) 프라이드(Pride)는 80년대 한국의 기아자동차에서 제작하여 판매한 대중적인 소형차이다.

The Margins, the Unwritten Blanks
Where Stories are Born

Jung Eun-kyoung (literary critic)

The story, "So Far, and Yet So Near," is a puzzle of sorts. The author throws out several fragmentary situations and then begins to fill in the connecting blanks as if assembling a detective novel. In doing so, he compels the reader to actively participate in the amusing task of filling in the blanks. With that being said, what exactly are these situations?

A. On April 6, 2004, Uncle disappeared after parking the Pride[1] next to the wall in front of our house.

1) The Pride is a popular compact car that was manufactured and sold in Korea by Kia Motors in the 1980's.

들을 위해 사준 것이다.

c. 삼촌이 사라진 후 나는 삼촌의 프라이드를 몰고 다녔다. 삼촌의 프라이드는 후진이 안 되기 때문에 밀어야 한다.

「밀수록 다시 가까워지는」은 위의 세 가지 풍경을 중심으로 이야기가 펼쳐진다. 그러니까 이 작품은 'a 2004년 삼촌 대신 남겨진 프라이드'라는 문제적 지점에서 이전의 대과거로 거슬러가는 'b의 지점', 그리고 이 모든 사건을 초점화하고 있는 현재적 나의 'c 시점', 이 세 고리를 오가며 진행되고 있는 것이다. 삼촌은 왜 사라졌는가? 프라이드는 왜 후진이 안 되는 걸까? 그 의문은 이야기되지 않은 '여백'의 자리이고, 이 여백에서 이야기는 시작된다. 또한 그것은 삼촌의 부재의 자리이기도 하다. 그리고 '부재와 여백'을 메꿔나가는 힘, 그 엔진은 곧 사랑과 그리움이다. '나'는 삼촌이 남긴 프라이드를 타고, 이 차에 남겨진 삼촌의 흔적을 좇아 1987년에서 2004년 사이를 오간다. 결코 온전히 메꿔질 수 없는, 구멍투성이의 '삼촌과 프라이드와 나'의 스토리를 정리하면 다음과 같다.

B. Grandmother bought Uncle the Pride in 1987 because he was still a bachelor.

C. After Uncle disappeared, I began driving the Pride. Because the Pride couldn't go in reverse, I had to push it.

"So Far, and Yet So Near" is a story that unfolds with these three situations at its core. The story hinges around these three points and then moves back and forth between them. The conflict of the story begins at point A, in 2004, when Uncle disappears after leaving his Pride. Then it shifts to the past perfect tense with point B, while all the while being recounted in the present by a first person narrator at point C. Why did Uncle disappear? Why doesn't the Pride go in reverse? The answers to these questions exist in the blanks of the story and it is from these unwritten spaces that the true story unfolds. These blanks also represent Uncle's absence within the story. The power that fills in the blanks and Uncle's absence, the driving forces of the story, is love and longing. The unnamed protagonist becomes the new driver of Uncle's Pride, and begins to chase the clues concerning his Uncle left in the car, traveling back and forth between

삼촌은 위의 형들 때문에 중학교만 졸업하고 농사를 짓던 농촌 총각이었다. 삼촌이 장가를 못 갈까봐 우려한 할머니는 삼촌을 서울로 올려보내고 서른 살의 삼촌은 구로동의 피혁공장에 다니게 된다. 그해 87년 할머니는 여자들을 꼬시라고 삼촌에게 프라이드를 사준다. 프라이드를 몰게 된 삼촌은 여자친구를 만들기는커녕 프라이드를 연인처럼 여기며 살아가게 되는데, 프라이드를 산 지 두 달 만에 공장을 그만두고 전국을 떠돌기 시작한다. 그 뒤 공사장 등지에서 일을 하면서 삼촌은 생계를 꾸렸고 가끔 집에 들른 삼촌은 방전된 프라이드를 밤새도록 꽉 끌어안고 있는 기이한 풍경을 연출하기도 한다. 그러던 2004년 4월 6일 삼촌은 18년 동안 47만 킬로를 주행했던 프라이드를 인감증명서, 주민등록초본과 함께 남기고 사라진다.

'나'는 할머니와 한 방을 쓰는 덕분에 할머니로부터 삼촌의 이야기를 많이 듣는다. 2004년 삼촌이 사라진 후 '나'는 삼촌의 프라이드를 몰고 다니게 된다. 그러는 동안 '나'는 삼촌의 흔적을 발견하게 되고 삼촌의 과거를 조금씩 알게 된다. 삼촌이 남긴 '차계부'와 단골 공업사를 통해 삼촌의 프라이드가 후진이 안 되는 것은 삼촌

1987 and 2004. Ultimately, the story of Uncle, the Pride, and the protagonist, remain full of holes, of blanks that cannot be entirely sealed. But even so, these are the facts we have.

The narrator's uncle has only finished junior high school and was left to take care of the farm as a lonely bachelor because of his two older brothers. Meanwhile Grandmother, who worried that Uncle would never get married, sends Uncle up to Seoul. Uncle, who is thirty at that time, gets a job at a leather factory in Guro-dong. That year, in 1987, Grandmother buys Uncle the Pride in order for him to attract girls. But even with a car, Uncle doesn't find a girlfriend but instead, carries on, treating the Pride as if it is his lover. Two months later, Uncle quits his job at the factory and begins to wander all over the country. He stays afloat by finding work at random construction sites, but on one of the few times he visits home, he displays a rash of alarming behavior when he stays up all night hugging the Pride after its battery accidentally ended up completely drained. Then, on April 6, 2004, he vanishes while leaving behind the Pride, which he has spent 18 years in and travelled 470,000km with. He also puts two copies of his authentication certificate of

이 처음부터 일부러 그렇게 만들었다는 것 등, 또 차계부에 '청주' '하동' 등이 자주 기록되고 있다는 것의 중요한 사실을 알게 된다. 이 수수께끼를 푸는 동안 '나'는 '삼촌'과 점점 가까워지게 되고, 또한 프라이드를 타고 대학원에 다니고 연애도 하면서 성장하게 된다.

'내가' 삼촌을 어렴풋하게 이해하게 된 것은, '고모'와 '고모부'를 통해 다음과 같은 일을 짐작하게 되면서부터이다. 삼촌은 87년 구로동 공장의 어느 모임에서 한 여자를 만나고 사랑하게 된다. 그 모임은 '구로동일꾼노동자회'였는데, 학출 출신들이 주축 멤버였던 이 모임은 당시 경찰서 공안계로부터 집중 감시를 받고 있었다. 경찰관인 '고모부'는 당시 이들의 기밀을 캐내기 위해 '고모'에게 '은행원'이라고 속이고 의도적으로 접근한다. 결국 이들은 국가보안법 위반혐의로 검거되고 삼촌이 좋아했던 여자는 감옥에 가게 된다. 삼촌은 '프라이드' 구입에 고모부의 돈이 어느 정도 들어있다는 사실을 알게 되고, 후진 패킹을 뺌으로써 '프락치'의 몫을 제거한다. 그리고 사랑했던 여자를 면회하기 위해 청주로, 그리고 '그녀'의 고향 하동으로 질주했던 것이다. '나'는 막연히 이끌려 '하동'에 가게 되고 그곳에서 '후진 안 되는

personal seal and his resident registration papers in the glove compartment.

Meanwhile the narrator ends up sharing a room with Grandmother and so is able to hear endless stories of his mystery Uncle. After Uncle disappears in 2004, the narrator begins to drive the Pride. As he drives the car, he uncovers clues left by Uncle and starts to learn of his uncle's past. From Uncle's "car-keeping ledger" and regular repair shop, the narrator learns that, since the beginning, the Pride had been unable to reverse because his uncle had deliberately removed a part from it. The narrator also finds an important clue when stumbling upon a list of locations in the car-keeping ledger, noting locations such as Cheongju and Hadong, which are repeatedly recorded. While figuring out the pieces of this puzzle, the narrator becomes closer to Uncle but also grows while driving the Pride, entering grad school and also beginning to date.

The narrator starts to get a better understanding of Uncle after he begins to hear stories of Auntie and her ex-husband. Of particular note, in 1987, the narrator learns his uncle had once been involved with an activist group at the Guro-dong factory and fell in love with one of its female mem-

프라이드'를 알고 있는 소녀를 만나고, 삼촌이 좋아했던 '그녀'에게 그만한 딸이 있다는 사실을 알게 된다. 그리고 돌아와 프라이드가 완전히 멈출 때까지 그 차를 몰고 다닌다. 그 사이 할머니는 폐암에 걸려 치료를 받고, 고모는 고모부와 이혼을 하고, 삼촌은 여전히 소식이 없다.

'나'는 위의 시간들을 거치면서 삼촌이 프라이드를 버린 것이 아니라 프라이드와 '이별'했음을 짐작하게 된다. 작가는 여기서 모든 이야기를 마치면서 여전히 여백을 독자들에게 남기고 있는데, 그 여백은 다음과 같은 말들을 품고 있을 것이다.

삼촌에게 1987년에서 2004년까지 18년 간 함께 한 프라이드는 사실, 그가 87년에 만난 '첫사랑 그 여자'와 같은 존재이다. 삼촌은 사랑으로 그리고 죄책감으로 오랜 세월 그녀를 찾아다녔을 것이고, 그러나 끝내 그녀와 행복해질 수 없었던 삼촌은 '프라이드'와 결별하고 사라져버린다. 연인을 대신한 '프라이드'의 이 각별함은 삼촌에게뿐 아니라 할머니에게도 마찬가지이다. 할머니에게 프라이드는 아들이어서 그 차가 여전히 '굴러다니길' 갈망한다. '나'에게도 마찬가지로 프라이드는 '삼촌'

bers. The "Guro-dong Workers Labor Union," consisting mostly of former college students, was under police surveillance by the public security division of the district police precinct. Auntie's ex-husband had been in charge of the investigation, and had pretended to be a bank clerk to deliberately approach Auntie in order to procure information about the group. The members were arrested under charges of violation of national security laws, and the narrator's uncle's mystery woman ends up going to jail. It was at this point that Uncle discovered that a portion of the Pride was paid for with money from his sister's ex-husband, and so he intentionally removes the rubber gasket of the Pride's reverse gear. By removing this critical component of his beloved car, he *removes* the "police infor mant" (*p'urakch'i/fraktsiya*) aspect of it as well. Uncle goes to Cheongju in search of the girl, and ultimately ends up racing all the way down to the girl's hometown in Hadong. Not knowing exactly why, the narrator travels to Hadong and there, he runs into a young girl who knows that the car cannot go in reverse. He finds out that Uncle's "girl" has a daughter who is about the same age as the young girl. The narrator returns to Seoul and continues

이고, 또 삼촌을 그리는 '할머니'이기도 하고, 또 삼촌이 품었을 '깊은 슬픔과 사랑'이기도 하고, 또 '내'가 새롭게 써나간 '사랑'이기도 했던 것이다. 그리하여 '나'는 이제 죽음을 앞둔 할머니와 함께 '이별식'을 치른다. '나'는 할머니를 더 이상 운행되지 않는 프라이드에 모시고 수동으로, 프라이드를 밀고 동네 한 바퀴를 돈다. 그것은 곧 '내'가 주례하는 할머니와 '삼촌'의 이별식, 혹은 '프라이드'의 장례라고 할 수 있다. 할머니는 이 애도의 순례 중에서 다음과 같이 말한다. "야, 야, 이러니까 꼭 옛날 생각난다. 옛날에 네 삼촌도 나랑 논일 끝내고 집으로 돌아올 때면 꼭 리어카를 이렇게 밀었거든. 끝지 않고, 꼭 뒤에서 밀었어. 이 할미 얼굴 계속 바라보면서 말이야……."

'밀수록 다시 가까워지는'이라는 제목은 할머니의 이 말, 곧 '밀면서 마주하게 된 얼굴'이라는 의미일 것이다. 그것은 '내'가 후진이 안 되는 프라이드를 밀면서 마주하게 된 삼촌의 얼굴이고, 연인 혹은 어머니의 얼굴, 즉 모든 사랑의 표정들인 것이다.

driving the Pride until it finally stops running. During all of this, the narrator's grandmother receives treatment for lung cancer, his aunt procures a divorce form her husband, and his uncle's whereabouts remain a mystery.

As the narrator moves through this timeline, he comes to the conclusion that Uncle didn't abandon the Pride but, rather, had "parted with it for good." This is the ending that the author leaves the reader with, still replete with blanks, but blanks that the reader can probably answer with the following possibilities.

To the narrator's uncle, the Pride, which he'd driven for 18 years from 1987 to 2004, is the same as his first love, a girl he'd met in 1987. Because of love, and also out of guilt, the narrator's uncle most likely spends years in search of her. However, because a happy ending for them is impossible, he chooses to part with "the Pride" and vanishes. The particular fondness the narrator's uncle feels towards the Pride as his lover is shared by the Grandmother. To the narrator's Grandmother, the Pride represents Uncle and so she desperately hopes that "it won't die." As for the narrator, the Pride was his Uncle, his grandmother's yearning for his uncle, the deep love and sorrow that his uncle had borne, as well as the new love being written by the narrator. In the end, the narrator holds a farewell ceremony with Grandmother, who is also nearing her death. He sits Grandmother in the passenger seat of the Pride, even though it no longer runs, and pushes it himself, taking the Pride for one final spin around the neighborhood. One might see this as the narrator officiating a farewell ceremony between Grandmother and Uncle, but one might also view this as the Pride's last funeral rites. During these mourning processions, then, Grandmother offers a final tender remark, "Hey, hey. Sitting here like this reminds me of long time ago. Back then, your Uncle would push me in the pushcart like this on our way home after finishing work in the fields. He wouldn't pull it. He'd always push it from the back, looking at my face."

This final scene probably explains the title, "So Far, and Yet So Near." Like Grandmother's words, "the longer you push, the closer you see the face." In other words, when the narrator pushes the Pride that remains unable to reverse, he sees the face of his uncle, the face of a lover or a mother, all the faces of love.

비평의 목소리

Critical Acclaim

이 나라 80년대 프라이드라 이름하는 명차가 있었다.
그것과 삼촌의 여사여사한 일들이 펼쳐지는 과정에서
작가는 이 시대를 살아온 자로서의 삼촌을 프라이드라
는 이름의 자동차로 둔갑시켰다. 그 자동차의 운명이
곧 삼촌의 운명이라는 것. 거기에는 반드시 '여백'이라
는 것이 있다는 것. 이 '여백'이 얘기 아닌 소설의 본질이
라는 것. 바로 여기가 할머니의 고담과 소설가의 소설
이 갈라지는 대목이다.

김윤식

삼촌의 차계부에는 삼촌으로서도 어찌할 수 없는 삶

The Pride was an actual car that was popular in Korea in the 80's. By writing a story about Uncle and the Pride, the author turns Uncle, also a character from that period, into the vehicle named Pride. The moment when the fate of the Pride becomes the fate of Uncle, the fact that an unwritten blank undoubtedly exists there, and the notion that this blank is not a part of the story but holds within it the essence of fiction—it is at this very point where the author's fiction separates itself from Grandmother's tale.

Kim Yun-shik

의 여백이 자리잡고 있다는 사실이다. 더더욱 분명한 것은 삼촌으로서도 어찌할 수 없는 삶의 여백은 어느 누군가에 의해서도 결코 이야기될 수 없다는 점이다. 삼촌이 차를 밀었던 만큼의 거리는, 기록되어 있지 않은 여백이거나 여백에 의해 씌어진 글쓰기이다. 어쩌면 한 번도 이야기될 수 없을지도 모르는 삶의 여백, 또는 어쩌면 결코 이야기될 수 없을지도 모르는 이야기의 여백, 삶과 이야기의 여백이 그 어떤 이야기를 들려주었던가. 이야기될 수 없는 삶이 스스로를 드러내지 않았겠는가. 삶과 이야기의 여백은 삼촌의 삶에서 어쩌면 가장 빛났을 순간을 다만 지시하고 있을 따름이다.

김동식

그는 결코 폼을 잡는 이야기꾼이기를 바라지 않는 것 같다. 누구보다도 이야기꾼이 어떤 존재였는지 잘 알고 있기 때문이다. 그는 장식으로서의 문학을 거부한다. 그는 활달한 이야기꾼이기를 소망한다. (…) 잡다한 레퍼토리를 가지고 그는 닦고 조이고 기름을 쳐서 제법 윤택한 이야기를 만들어낸다. 폼 잡으며 거론하는 서사의 종론 담론 따위를 슬며시 조소한다. 이기호, 그에게

Uncle's car-keeping ledger shows that life contains blanks that even he can't fill in. What's clearer is that these blanks, the stories within these blank, are incapable of being told by anybody else. The distances that Uncle travelled while pushing the car are either blanks that were left unwritten, or the ledger itself was written by these blanks. The stories within the blanks in life may never be told, or even the stories within Uncle's story can never be told. When has a blank within life or a story ever revealed its tale? If it was possible, then wouldn't it have revealed itself already? But the blanks in Uncle's life and the blanks in his story simply control the most glorious moments in Uncle's life.

Kim Dong-shik

Ultimately, it doesn't seem like he wants to be a pretentious storyteller. This is because he knows better than anybody else what storytellers used to be. He rejects literature as ornamentation. He wants to be a diverse storyteller. [...] With his own diverse array or repertoire of narrative techniques, he polishes, tightens, and slicks his stories to a shine. He quietly scoffs at the pretentious discourses regarding narrations. To Lee Ki-ho, there

이야기의 바깥은 없다.

우찬제

　그는 '개념 없는' 작가다. 소설가라면 반드시 갖춰야
할 개념들이 있다. '소설(가)'에 대한 개념, '인물'에 대한
개념, '역사'에 대한 개념이 그것이다. 소설 혹은 소설가
란 모름지기 이러저러해야 한다는 개념들이 엄연하지
만 그에게는 별무소용이다. 소설의 인물들이 비루해지
기 시작한 것은 90년대 이후의 한 흐름이지만 이 작가
의 인물들에게는 때로 비루하다는 말조차 과분하다. 역
사를 대하는 태도도 용감하다. 그는 때로 '역사(History)'
를 '안녕, 이야기!(Hi, Story)'의 합성어 정도로 생각하는
것처럼 보인다. 좋다는 이야기다. 그는 개념 없는 아담
의 눈으로 인간을 관찰하고 세상을 읽는다. 무구한 아
담의 목소리로 눈치 없이 이야기를 늘어놓는다. 덕분에
그의 소설에서는 못 할 일이 없고 안 되는 일이 없다. 절
대적으로 악한 것도 절대적으로 선한 것도 없다.

신형철

　이기호의 소설은 거대한 (큰)타자, 혹은 항상—이미

is nothing outside the story.   Woo Chan-je

He is an author who subscribes to no defining narrative concepts. As a novelist, there are certain concepts that you must have. Concepts of the author, concepts of the characters, and concepts of history. These are the concepts. As a work of fiction or as a writer of fiction, there are various conceits that one must follow, but this doesn't apply to him. Vulgar characters were a trend in fiction that started after the 90's, but at times, for this author's characters, the word "vulgar" is too generous. Even the way he treats history is courageous. Sometimes, it seems like he regards the word "History" as merely a compound of the words "Hi" and "story," i.e. "Hi, Story!" But all of this is what makes him great. He observes people and reads the world through the eyes of an Adam free from the constraints of artistic conceits. Then in the naïve voice of Adam, he gives free will to his writing. Because of this, there is nothing he can't do or say in his works. His works are void of anything absolutely evil or absolutely pure.

                                         Shin Hyeong-cheol

'나'를 제약하는 타자의 질서에 대한 문학적 인식과 태도를 출발점으로 하는 2000년대 문학의 한 상징이기도 하고, 계몽과 고백이라는 이제까지 한국문학의 화법과는 전혀 다른 '90년대 이후'의 화자인 탈내향적 1인칭 화자 혹은 '골빈 화자'의 개인적 방언을 구현한 소설로도 칭해진다. 또 그런가 하면 이기호의 소설은 90년대 이후 한국에 도래한 부르주아 모더니티에 맞서 이야기, 망상, 기존의 권위주의적 담론 등을 한자리에 모아 '미친, 새로운' 소설의 제국주의를 건설하는 데 성공한, 그러니까 주변의 모든 장르들을 병합하는 이질혼종적인 소설의 제국을 훌륭하게 구축한 경우로 칭해지기도 하고, 또 아비가 부재한 2000년대 세대의 특성을 고스란히 공유하는 소설로도 규정된다. 그 맥락이야 어떠하건 이기호의 소설은 '90년대 이후' 혹은 2000년대 한국문학의 한 경향, 혹은 징후로서 읽히고 자리매겨진 것이 사실이다.

류보선

Lee Ki-ho's fiction represents the literature of the year 2000. Whether his writing is grand and loud or always controlled by a limiting unnamed "I," the starting point of all his work is his literary awareness and attitude regarding order. Contrary to the narrative voices in the post-'90's Korean literary scene that dealt so much with enlightenment and confession, his works include masked introverted narrators who speak in the first person, or "empty-headed" narrators who ramble alone. At the same time, his fiction challenges the bourgeois modernity that made its way into post-'90's Korea and by gathering together story, delusion, and the existing authoritarian discourse, he succeeds in constructing an imperialistic type of fiction that is "crazy" and "fresh." In other words, one can describe his fiction as a merger of all genres; a brilliant hybrid construction. One might also hail his works as completely sharing the characteristics of the 2000's generation's views regarding the absent father. Regardless of the context, it's an undeniable fact that one should consider Lee Ki-ho's fiction an omen or harbinger of the next trend in post-'90's or perhaps, even millennial Korean literature.

Ryu Bo-sun

이기호

1972년 강원도 원주에서 태어나 추계예대 문예창작학
과를 졸업했다. 1999년《현대문학》신인추천공모에 단
편「버니」가 당선되어 작품 활동을 시작했다. 소설집
『최순덕 성령충만기』『갈팡질팡하다가 내 이럴 줄 알았
지』『김 박사는 누구인가?』, 장편소설『사과는 잘해요』
등을 펴냈고, 2010년 단편「밀수록 다시 가까워지는」으
로 이효석문학상을 수상했다. 현재 광주대 문예창작학
과에서 교수로 재직하고 있다.

Lee Ki-ho

Lee Ki-ho was born in Wonju, Gangwon-do in 1972 and graduated from the Chugye University for the Arts in creative writing. Lee Ki-ho made his literary debut when his short story "Bunny" won the monthly *Hyundae Munhak* New Writer's Contest in 1999. He has produced three short story collections, *Choi Sunduk Full of the Holy Spirit*; *Fumbling, I Knew I'd End Up Like This*; and *Who is Dr. Kim*. He had also written a full length novel, *At Least We Can Apologize*. In 2010, he won the Yi Hyo-seok Literature Award for his short story, "So Far, and Yet So Near." He is currently a professor in the department of creative writing at Gwangju University.

번역 **테레사 김** Translated by Teresa Kim

테레사 김(김수진)은 캐나다 브리티시컬럼비아 대학교에서 영문학 과정 중에 브루스 풀턴 교수의 지도하에 한국 현대문학 공부를 시작하였다. 2010년에 한국문학번역원(KLTI)에서 정규과정을 수료함으로써 본격적인 문학 번역 활동을 시작하였다. 브리티시 컬럼비아 대학교와 서울대학교에서 공동 개최되는 한국문학번역워크숍에서 박완서의 『부끄러움을 가르칩니다』라는 작품으로 수상하였고, 이후 2010년과 2013년에 서울에서 열린 워크숍에도 참여하였다. 『부끄러움을 가르칩니다』는 문학잡지 《ACTA KOREANA》와 한국현대문학 단편소설집 「WAXEN WINGS」에 발간되었고 이후 우애령의 「와인 바에서」, 김경욱의 「위험한 독서」, 그리고 윤성희의 「부메랑」을 번역하였다. 부산 영화 포럼에서 부산영화제 자료를 번역하였고 국제교류진흥회(ICF)에서 영문 웹사이트와 자료를 번역하였다. 최근에는 한국영상자료원에서 임권택, 신상옥, 김기덕 감독의 DVD 컬렉션을 번역하였다. 현재 서울에서 거주하며 프리랜서 번역가로 활동 중이다.

Teresa Kim completed her studies in English Literature at the University of British Columbia. Under the mentorship of Professor Bruce Fulton, she began her studies in Korean Literature translation while doing her undergrad and in 2010, she was chosen as a scholarship recipient to complete the English language translation program at the Korea Literature Translation Institute (KLTI). Upon completion of the program, she currently resides in Seoul as a freelance translator. She was an award recipient at the 2nd Annual Translation Seminar hosted by the University of British Columbia for the translation of "We Teach Shame!"and was also chosen to participate at the 3rd Annual Korean Literature Translation Workshop at Seoul National University in October 2010. In June 2013, she was invited to sit in on the 2013 Korean Literature Translation Workshop held at Seoul National University as an advising translator. Her translation of Park Wan-seo's short story, "We Teach Shame!"has been published in the literary magazine *ACTA KOREANA* and in the short story collection of modern Korean literature, *WAXEN WINGS*. She has also translated "At the Wine Bar" by Woo Ae-ryung, "A Dangerous Reading" by Kim Gyeong-uk, and "Boomerang" by Yun Seong-hui. As a freelance translator, she has worked with the Busan Cinema Forum for material related to the Busan Film Festival, for the International Communication Foundation (ICF) for the translation of their English website and annual reports, and most recently, she has worked with the Korea Film Archive (KOFA) for the translation of the DVD box collections for directors Im Kwon-taek, Shin Sang-ok, and Kim Kee-duk.

감수 **전승희, 데이비드 윌리엄 홍**

Translated by Jeon Seung-hee and David William Hong

전승희는 서울대학교와 하버드대학교에서 영문학과 비교문학으로 박사 학위를 받았으며, 현재 하버드대학교 한국학 연구소의 연구원으로 재직하며 아시아 문예 계간지 《ASIA》 편집위원으로 활동 중이다. 현대 한국문학 및 세계문학을 다룬 논문을 다수 발표했으며, 바흐친의 『장편소설과 민중언어』, 제인 오스틴의 『오만과 편견』 등을 공역했다. 1988년 한국여성연구소의 창립과 《여성과 사회》의 창간에 참여했고, 2002년부터 보스턴 지역 피학대 여성을 위한 단체인 '트랜지션하우스' 운영에 참여해 왔다. 2006년 하버드대학교 한국학 연구소에서 '한국 현대사와 기억'을 주제로 한 워크숍을 주관했다.

Jeon Seung-hee is a member of the Editorial Board of *ASIA*, and a Fellow at the Korea Institute, Harvard University. She received a Ph.D. in English Literature from Seoul National University and a Ph.D. in Comparative Literature from Harvard University. She has presented and published numerous papers on modern Korean and world literature. She is also a co-translator of Mikhail Bakhtin's *Novel and the People's Culture* and Jane Austen's *Pride and Prejudice*. She is a founding member of the Korean Women's Studies Institute and of the biannual Women's Studies' journal *Women and Society* (1988), and she has been working at 'Transition House,' the first and oldest shelter for battered women in New England. She organized a workshop entitled "The Politics of Memory in Modern Korea" at the Korea Institute, Harvard University, in 2006. She also served as an advising committee member for the Asia-Africa Literature Festival in 2007 and for the POSCO Asian Literature Forum in 2008.

데이비드 윌리엄 홍은 미국 일리노이주 시카고에서 태어났다. 일리노이대학교에서 영문학을, 뉴욕대학교에서 영어교육을 공부했다. 지난 2년간 서울에 거주하면서 처음으로 한국인과 아시아계 미국인 문학에 깊이 몰두할 기회를 가졌다. 현재 뉴욕에서 거주하며 강의와 저술 활동을 한다.

David William Hong was born in 1986 in Chicago, Illinois. He studied English Literature at the University of Illinois and English Education at New York University. For the past two years, he lived in Seoul, South Korea, where he was able to immerse himself in Korean and Asian-American literature for the first time. Currently, he lives in New York City, teaching and writing.

바이링궐 에디션 한국 대표 소설 058

밀수록 다시 가까워지는

2014년 3월 7일 초판 1쇄 인쇄 | 2014년 3월 14일 초판 1쇄 발행

지은이 이기호 | **옮긴이** 테레사 김 | **펴낸이** 김재범
감수 전승희, 데이비드 윌리엄 홍 | **기획** 정은경, 전성태, 이경재
편집 정수인, 이은혜 | **관리** 박신영 | **디자인** 이춘희
펴낸곳 (주)아시아 | **출판등록** 2006년 1월 27일 제406-2006-000004호
주소 서울특별시 동작구 서달로 161-1(흑석동 100-16)
전화 02.821.5055 | **팩스** 02.821.5057 | **홈페이지** www.bookasia.org
ISBN 979-11-5662-002-0 (set) | 979-11-5662-015-0 (04810)
값은 뒤표지에 있습니다.

Bi-lingual Edition Modern Korean Literature 058

So Far, and Yet So Near

Written by Lee Ki-ho | **Translated by** Teresa Kim
Published by Asia Publishers | 161-1, Seodal-ro, Dongjak-gu, Seoul, Korea
Homepage Address www.bookasia.org | **Tel.** (822).821.5055 | **Fax.** (822).821.5057
First published in Korea by Asia Publishers 2014
ISBN 979-11-5662-002-0 (set) | 979-11-5662-015-0 (04810)